# The Dark Side

## Truly Terrifying Tales

Title Withdrawn

Chosen by
Susan Price

KINGFISHER
BOSTON

NOV '07

KINGFISHER
a Houghton Mifflin Company imprint
222 Berkeley Street
Boston, Massachusetts 02116
www.houghtonmifflinbooks.com

First published in 1995
This edition published in 2007
2 4 6 8 10 9 7 5 3 1

LIBRARY OF CONGRESS CATALOGING–IN–PUBLICATION DATA
has been applied for.

ISBN 978-0-7534-6143-3

Printed in China
1TR/0507/PROSP/MAR/70NEWSP/C

# CONTENTS

chapter

# THE KIT BAG

## ALGERNON BLACKWOOD

WHEN THE WORDS "not guilty" sounded through the crowded courtroom that dark December afternoon, Arthur Wilbraham, the great criminal K.C. [king's counsel] and leader for the triumphant defense, was represented by his junior; but Johnson, his private secretary, carried the verdict across to his chambers like lightning.

"It's what we expected, I think," said the lawyer, without emotion; "and, personally, I am glad the case is over." There was no particular sign of pleasure that his defense of John Turk, the murderer, on a plea of insanity, had been successful, for no doubt he felt, as everybody who had watched the case felt, that no man had ever better deserved the gallows.

"I'm glad too," said Johnson. He had sat in the court for ten days watching the face of the man who had carried out with callous detail one of the most brutal and cold-blooded murders of recent years.

The counsel glanced up at his secretary. They were more than employer and employed; for family and other reasons, they were friends. "Ah, I remember; yes," he said with a kind smile, "and you want to get away for Christmas? You're going to skate and ski in the Alps, aren't you? If I was your age, I'd come with you."

Johnson laughed shortly. He was a young man of 26, with a delicate face like a girl's. "I can catch the morning boat now," he said, "but that's not the reason I'm glad the trial is over. I'm glad it's over because I've seen the last of that man's dreadful face. It positively haunted me. That white skin, with the black hair brushed low over the forehead, is a thing I shall never forget, and the description of the way the dismembered body was crammed and packed with lime into that—"

"Don't dwell on it, my dear fellow," interrupted the other, looking at him curiously out of his keen eyes. "Don't think about it. Such pictures have a trick of coming back when one least wants them." He paused a moment. "Now go," he added presently, "and enjoy your holiday. I shall want all of your energy for my Parliamentary work when you get back. And don't break your neck skiing."

Johnson shook hands and took his leave. At the door he turned suddenly.

"I knew there was something I wanted to ask you," he said. "Would you mind lending me one of your kit bags? It's too late to get one tonight, and I leave in the morning before the shops are open."

"Of course; I'll send Henry over with it to your rooms. You shall have it the moment I get home."

"I promise to take great care of it," said Johnson gratefully, delighted to think that within 30 hours he would be nearing the brilliant sunshine of the high Alps in the winter. The thought of that criminal court was like an evil dream in his mind.

He dined at his club and went on to Bloomsbury, where he occupied the top floor in one of those old, gaunt houses in which the rooms are large and lofty. The floor below his own was vacant and unfurnished, and below that were other lodgers whom he did not know. It was cheerless, and he heartily looked forward to a change. The night was even more cheerless: it was miserable, and few people were around. A cold, sleety rain was driving down the streets before the keenest east wind that he had ever felt. It howled dismally among the big, gloomy houses of the great squares, and when he reached his rooms, he heard it whistling and shouting over the world of black roofs beyond his windows.

In the hall he met his landlady, shading a candle from the drafts with her thin hand. "This come by a man from Mr. Wilbr'am's, sir."

She pointed to what was evidently the kit bag, and Johnson thanked her and took it upstairs with him. "I shall be going abroad in the morning for ten days, Mrs. Monks," he said. "I'll leave an address for letters."

"And I hope you'll 'ave a merry Christmas, sir," she said in a raucous, wheezy voice that suggested spirits, "and better weather than this."

"I hope so too," replied her lodger, shuddering a little as the wind went roaring down the street outside.

When he got upstairs, he heard the sleet volleying against the windowpanes. He put his kettle on to make a cup of hot coffee and then set about putting a few things in order for his absence

"And now I must pack—such as my packing is." He laughed to himself and set to work at once.

He liked the packing, for it brought the snow mountains so vividly before him and made him forget the unpleasant scenes of the past ten days. Besides, it was not elaborate in nature. His friend had lent him the very thing—a stout canvas kit bag, sack-shaped, with holes around the neck for the brass bar and padlock. It was a bit shapeless, true, and not much to look at, but its capacity was unlimited, and there was no need to pack carefully. He shoved in his waterproof coat, his fur cap and gloves, his skates and climbing boots, his sweaters, snow boots, and earmuffs; and then on the top of these he piled his woolen shirts and underwear, his thick socks, puttees, and knickerbockers. The dress suit came next, in case the hotel people dressed up for dinner, and then, thinking of the best way to pack his white shirts, he paused a moment to reflect. "That's the worst of these kit bags," he mused vaguely, standing in the center of the sitting room, where he had come to fetch some string.

It was after ten o'clock. A furious gust of wind rattled the windows as though to hurry him up, and he thought with pity of the poor Londoners whose Christmas would be spent in such a climate, while he was skimming over snowy slopes in bright sunshine and dancing in the evening with rosy-cheeked girls—ah! That reminded him; he must put in his dancing pumps and evening socks. He crossed over from his sitting room to the cupboard on the landing where he kept his linen.

And as he did so, he heard someone coming softly up the stairs.

He stood still a moment on the landing to listen. It was Mrs. Monks's step, he thought; she must be coming up with the last mail. But then the steps ceased suddenly, and he heard no more. They were at least two flights down, and he came to the conclusion that they were too heavy to be those of his bibulous landlady. No doubt they belonged to a late lodger who had mistaken his floor. He went into his bedroom and packed his pumps and dress shirts as best he could.

The kit bag by this time was two thirds full and stood upright on its own base like a sack of flour. For the first time he noticed that it was old and dirty, the canvas faded and worn, and that it had obviously been subjected to rather rough treatment. It was not a very nice bag to have sent him—certainly not a new one or one that his chief valued. He gave the matter a passing thought and went on with his packing. Once or twice, however, he caught himself wondering who it could have been wandering down below, for Mrs. Monks had not come up with letters, and the floor was empty and unfurnished. From time to time, moreover, he was almost certain that he heard a soft tread of someone padding around over the bare boards—cautiously, stealthily, as silently as possible—and, further, that the sounds had been lately coming distinctly closer.

For the first time in his life he began to feel a little creepy. Then, as though to emphasize this feeling, an odd thing happened: as he left the bedroom, having just packed his recalcitrant white shirts, he noticed that the top of the kit bag lopped over toward him with an extraordinary resemblance to a human face. The canvas fell into a fold like a nose and forehead, and the brass rings for the padlock just filled the position of the eyes. A shadow—or was it a travel stain? for he could not tell exactly—looked like hair. It gave him rather a shock, for it was so absurdly, so outrageously, like the face of John Turk, the murderer.

He laughed and went into the front room, where the light was stronger.

*That horrid case has gotten on my mind*, he thought; *I shall be glad of a change of scene and air.* In the sitting room, however, he was not pleased to hear again that stealthy tread upon the stairs and to realize that it was much closer than before, as well as unmistakably real. And this time he got up and went out to see who it could be creeping around on the upper staircase at so late an hour.

But the sound ceased; there was no one visible on the stairs. He went to the floor below, not without trepidation, and turned on the electric light to make sure that no one was hiding in the empty rooms of the unoccupied suite. There was not a stick of furniture large enough to hide a dog. Then he called over the banisters to Mrs. Monks, but there was no answer, and his voice echoed down into the dark vault of the house and was lost in the roar of the gale that howled outside. Everyone was in bed and asleep—everyone except himself and the owner of this soft and stealthy tread.

*My absurd imagination, I suppose,* he thought. *It must have been the wind after all, although—it seemed so very real and close, I thought.* He went back to his packing. It was by this time getting on toward midnight. He drank his coffee and lit another pipe—the last before turning in.

It is difficult to say exactly at what point fear begins, when the causes of that fear are not plainly before the eyes. Impressions gather on the surface of the mind, film by film, as ice gathers on the surface of still water, but often so lightly that they claim no definite recognition from the consciousness. Then a point is reached where the accumulated impressions become a definite emotion, and the mind realizes that something has happened. With something of a start, Johnson suddenly recognized that he felt nervous—oddly nervous; also, that for some time past the causes of this feeling had been gathering slowly in his mind, but that he had only just reached the point where he was forced to acknowledge them.

It was a singular and curious malaise that had come over him, and he hardly knew what to make of it. He felt as though he was doing something that was strongly objected to by another person, another person, moreover, who had some right to object. It was a most disturbing and disagreeable feeling, not unlike the persistent promptings of conscience: almost, in fact, as if he was doing something that he knew to be wrong. Yet, though he searched vigorously and honestly in his mind, he could nowhere lay his finger upon the secret of this growing uneasiness, and it perplexed him. More, it distressed and frightened him.

"Pure nerves, I suppose," he said aloud with a forced laugh. "Mountain air will cure all that! Ah," he added, still speaking to himself, "and that reminds me—my snow glasses."

He was standing by the door of the bedroom during this brief soliloquy, and as he passed quickly toward the sitting room to fetch them from the cupboard, he saw out of the corner of his eye the indistinct outline of a figure standing on the stairs, a few feet from the top. It was someone in a stooping position, with one hand on the banister and the face peering up toward the landing. And at the same moment he heard a shuffling footstep. The person who had been creeping around below all this time had at last come up to his own floor. Who in the world could it be? And what in the name of heaven did he want?

Johnson caught his breath sharply and stood stock-still. Then, after a few seconds hesitation, he found his courage and turned to investigate. The stairs, he saw to his utter amazement, were empty; there was no one. He felt a series of cold shivers run over him, and something around the muscles of his legs gave a little and grew weak. For the space of several minutes he peered steadily into the shadows that congregated around the top of the staircase where he had seen the figure, and then he walked fast— almost ran, in fact—into the light of the front room; but hardly had he passed inside the doorway when he heard someone come up the stairs behind him with a quick bound and go swiftly into his bedroom. It was a heavy, but at the same time a stealthy, footstep—the tread of somebody who did not wish to be seen. And it was at this precise moment that the nervousness he had hitherto experienced leaped the boundary line and entered the state of fear, almost of acute, unreasoning fear. Before it turned into terror there was a further boundary to cross, and beyond that again lay the region of pure horror. Johnson's position was an unenviable one.

"By Jove! That *was* someone on the stairs, then," he muttered, his flesh crawling all over; "and whoever it was has now gone into my bedroom." His delicate, pale face turned absolutely white, and for some minutes he hardly knew what to think or do. Then he realized intuitively that delay only set a premium upon fear; and he crossed the landing boldly and went straight into the other room, where, a few seconds before, the steps had disappeared.

"Who's there? Is that you, Mrs. Monks?" he called aloud as he went, and he heard the first half of his words echo down the empty stairs, while the second half fell dead against the curtains in a room that apparently held no other human figure than his own.

"Who's there?" he called again in a voice unnecessarily loud and that only just held firm. "What do you want here?"

The curtains swayed very slightly, and, as he saw it, his heart felt as if it almost missed a beat; yet he dashed forward and drew them aside with a rush. A window, streaming with rain, was all that met his gaze. He continued his search, but in vain; the cupboards held nothing but rows of clothes, hanging motionless; and under the bed there was no sign of anyone hiding. He stepped backward into the middle of the room, and, as he did so, something all but tripped him up. Turning with a sudden spring of alarm he saw—the kit bag.

*Odd!* he thought. *That's not where I left it!* A few moments before it had surely been on his right, between the bed and the bathtub; he did not remember having moved it. It was very curious. What in the world was the matter with everything? Had all of his senses gone queer? A terrific gust of wind tore at the windows, dashing the sleet against the glass with the force of a small gunshot, and then fled away, howling dismally over the waste of Bloomsbury roofs. A sudden vision of the English Channel the next day rose in his mind and recalled him sharply to realities.

"There's no one here at any rate; that's quite clear!" he exclaimed aloud. Yet at the time he uttered them he knew perfectly well that his words were not true and that he did not believe them himself. He felt exactly as though someone was hiding close to him, watching all of his movements, trying to hinder his packing in some way. "And two of my senses," he added, keeping up the pretense, "have played me the most absurd tricks: the steps I heard and the figure I saw were both entirely imaginary."

He went back to the front room, poked the fire into a blaze, and sat down before it to think. What impressed him more than anything else was the fact that the kit bag was no longer where he had left it. It had been dragged closer to the door.

What happened afterward that night happened, of course, to a man already excited by fear and was perceived by a mind that had not the full and proper control, therefore, of the senses. Outwardly, Johnson remained calm and a master of himself to the end, pretending to the very last that everything he witnessed had a natural explanation or was merely delusions of his tired nerves. But inwardly, in his very heart, he knew all along that someone had been hiding downstairs in the empty suite when he came in, that this person had watched for his opportunity and then stealthily made his way up to the bedroom, and that all he saw and heard afterward, from the moving of the kit bag to—well, to the other things that this story has to tell—were caused directly by the presence of this invisible person.

And it was here, just when he most desired to keep his mind and thoughts controlled, that the vivid pictures received day after day upon the mental plates exposed in the courtroom of the Old Bailey came strongly to light and developed themselves in the darkroom of his inner vision. Unpleasant, haunting memories have a way of coming to life again just when the mind least desires them—in the silent watches of the night, on sleepless pillows, during the lonely hours spent by sick and dying beds. And so now, in the same way, Johnson saw nothing but the dreadful face of John Turk, the murderer, lowering at him from every corner of his mental field of vision: the white skin, the evil eyes, and the fringe of black hair low over the forehead. All of the pictures of those ten days in court crowded back into his mind unbidden and very vivid.

"This is all rubbish and nerves," he exclaimed at length, springing with sudden energy from his chair. "I shall finish my packing and go to bed. I'm overwrought, overtired. No doubt, at this rate I shall hear steps and things all night!"

But his face was deadly white all the same. He snatched up his field glasses and walked across to the bedroom, humming a music-hall song as he went—a trifle too loud to be natural; and the instant he crossed the threshold and stood within the room something turned cold around his heart, and he felt that every hair on his head stood up.

The kit bag lay close in front of him, several feet closer to the door than he had left it, and just over its crumpled top he saw a head and face slowly sinking down out of sight as though someone was crouching behind it to hide, and at the same moment a sound like a long-drawn sigh was distinctly audible in the still air around him between the gusts of the storm outside.

Johnson had more courage and willpower than the girlish indecision of his face indicated; but at first such a wave of terror came over him that for some seconds he could do nothing but stand and stare. A violent trembling ran down his back and legs, and he was conscious of a foolish, almost an hysterical, impulse to scream aloud. That sigh seemed in his very ear, and the air still quivered with it. It was unmistakably a human sigh.

"Who's there?" he said at length, finding his voice; but though he meant to speak with loud decision, the tones came out instead in a faint whisper, for he had partly lost the control of his tongue and lips.

He stepped forward so that he could see all around and over the kit bag. Of course there was nothing there, nothing but the faded carpet and the bulging canvas sides. He put out his hands and threw open the mouth of the sack where it had fallen over, being only three parts full, and then he saw for the first time that around the inside, some six inches from the top, there ran a broad smear of dull crimson. It was an old and faded bloodstain. He uttered a scream and drew back his hands as if they had been burned. At the same moment the kit bag gave a faint, but unmistakable, lurch forward toward the door.

Johnson collapsed backward, searching with his hands for the support of something solid, and the door, being farther behind him than he realized, received his weight just in time to prevent his falling and shut with a resounding bang. At the same moment the swinging of his left arm accidentally touched the electric switch, and the light in the room went out.

It was an awkward and disagreeable predicament, and if Johnson had not been possessed of real pluck, he might have done all manner of foolish things. As it was, however, he pulled himself together and groped furiously for the little brass knob to turn the light on again. But the rapid closing of the door had set the coats hanging on it swinging, and his fingers became entangled in a confusion of sleeves and pockets so that it was some moments before he found the switch. And in those few moments of bewilderment and terror two things happened that sent him beyond recall over the boundary into the region of genuine horror: he distinctly heard the kit bag shuffling heavily across the floor in jerks, and close in front of his face sounded once again the sigh of a human being.

\In his anguished efforts to find the brass button on the wall, he almost scraped the nails from his fingers, but even then, in those frenzied moments of alarm—so swift and alert are the impressions of a mind keyed up by a vivid emotion—he had time to realize that he dreaded the return of the light and that it might be better for him to stay hidden in the merciful screen of darkness. It was but the impulse of a moment, however, and before he had time to act upon it, he had yielded automatically to the original desire, and the room was flooded again with light.

But the second instinct had been right. It would have been better for him to have stayed in the shelter of the kind darkness. For there, close before him, bending over the half-packed kit bag, as clear as life in the merciless glare of the electric light, stood the figure of John Turk, the murderer. Not three feet from him the man stood, the fringe of black hair marked plainly against the pallor of the forehead, the whole horrible presentment of the scoundrel, as vivid as he had seen him day after day in the Old Bailey, when he stood there in the dock, cynical and callous, under the very shadow of the gallows.

In a flash Johnson realized what it all meant: the dirty and much-used bag; the smear of crimson within the top; the dreadful stretched condition of the bulging sides. He remembered how the victim's body had been stuffed inside a canvas bag for burial, the ghastly, dismembered fragments forced with lime into this very bag, and the bag itself produced as evidence—it all came back to him as clear as day . . .

Very softly and stealthily his hand groped behind him for the handle of the door, but before he could actually turn it, the very thing that he most of all dreaded came about, and John Turk lifted his devil's face and looked at him. At the same moment that heavy sigh passed through the air of the room, formulated somehow into words: "It's my bag. And I want it."

Johnson just remembered clawing open the door and then falling in a heap upon the floor of the landing as he tried frantically to make his way into the front room.

He remained unconscious for a long time, and it was still dark when he opened his eyes and realized that he was lying, stiff and bruised, on the cold boards. Then the memory of what he had seen rushed back into his mind, and he promptly fainted again. When he woke the second time, the wintry dawn was just beginning to peep in at the windows, painting the stairs a cheerless, dismal gray, and he managed to crawl into the front room and cover himself with an overcoat in the armchair, where at length he fell asleep.

A great clamor woke him. He recognized Mrs. Monks's voice, loud and voluble.

"What! You ain't been to bed, sir! Are you ill, or has anything 'appened? And there's an urgent gentleman to see you, though it ain't seven o'clock yet, and—"

"Who is it?" he stammered. "I'm all right, thanks. Fell asleep in my chair, I suppose."

"Someone from Mr. Wilb'ram's, and he says he ought to see you quick before you go abroad, and I told him—"

"Show him up, please, at once," said Johnson, whose head was whirling, and his mind was still full of dreadful visions.

Mr. Wilbraham's man came in with many apologies and explained briefly and quickly that an absurd mistake had been made and that the wrong kit bag had been sent over the night before.

"Henry somehow got hold of the one that came over from the courtroom, and Mr. Wilbraham only discovered it when he saw his own lying in his room and asked why it had not gone to you," the man said.

"Oh!" said Johnson stupidly.

"And he must have brought you the one from the murder case instead, sir, I'm afraid," the man continued, without the ghost of an expression on his face. "The one John Turk packed the dead body in. Mr. Wilbraham's awful upset about it, sir, and told me to come over first thing this morning with the right one, as you were leaving by the boat."

He pointed to a clean-looking kit bag on the floor, which he had just brought. "And I was to bring the other one back, sir," he added casually.

For some minutes Johnson could not find his voice. At last he pointed in the direction of his bedroom. "Perhaps you would kindly unpack it for me. Just empty the things out on the floor."

The man disappeared into the other room and was gone for five minutes. Johnson heard the shifting to and fro of the bag and the rattle of the skates and boots being unpacked.

"Thank you, sir," the man said, returning with the bag folded over his arm. "And can I do anything more to help you, sir?"

"What is it?" asked Johnson, seeing that he still had something that he wished to say.

The man shuffled and looked mysterious. "Beg pardon, sir, but knowing your interest in the Turk case, I thought you'd maybe like to know what's happened—"

"Yes."

"John Turk killed himself last night with poison immediately on getting his release, and he left a note for Mr. Wilbraham saying as he'd be much obliged if they'd have him put away, same as the woman he murdered, in the old kit bag."

"What time—did he do it?" asked Johnson.

"Ten o'clock last night, sir, the warden says."

# HERE THERE BE TYGERS

STEPHEN KING

CHARLES NEEDED TO go to the bathroom very badly.

There was no longer any use in trying to fool himself that he could wait for recess. His bladder was screaming at him, and Miss Bird had caught him squirming.

There were three third-grade teachers at the Acorn Street Grammar School. Miss Kinney was young and blonde and bouncy and had a boyfriend who picked her up after school in a blue Camaro. Mrs. Trask was shaped like a Moorish pillow and did her hair in braids and laughed boomingly. And there was Miss Bird.

Charles had known that he would end up with Miss Bird. He had *known* that. It had been inevitable. Because Miss Bird obviously wanted to destroy him. She did not allow children to go to the basement. The basement, Miss Bird said, was where the boilers were kept, and well-groomed ladies and gentlemen would never go down *there*, because basements were nasty, sooty old things. Young ladies and gentlemen do not go to the basement, she said. They go to the *bathroom*.

Charles squirmed again.

Miss Bird cocked an eye at him. "Charles," she said clearly, still pointing her pointer at Bolivia, "do you need to go to the bathroom?"

Cathy Scott in the seat ahead of him giggled, wisely covering her mouth.

Kenny Griffen snickered and kicked Charles under his desk.

Charles turned bright red.

"Speak up, Charles," Miss Bird said brightly. "Do you need to—"

(*urinate, she'll say urinate, she always does*)

"Yes, Miss Bird."

"Yes, what?"

"I have to go to the base—to the bathroom."

Miss Bird smiled. "Very well, Charles. You may go to the bathroom and urinate. Is that what you need to do? Urinate?"

Charles hung his head, convicted.

"Very well, Charles. You may do so. And next time kindly don't wait to be asked."

General giggles. Miss Bird rapped the board with her pointer.

Charles trudged up the row toward the door, 30 pairs of eyes boring into his back, and every one of those kids, including Cathy Scott, knew that he was going to the bathroom to urinate. The door was at least a football field's length away. Miss Bird did not go on with the lesson, but kept her silence until he had opened the door, entered the blessedly empty hall, and shut the door again.

He walked down toward the boys' bathroom,

(*basement basement basement IF I WANT*)
dragging his fingers along the cool tile of the wall, letting them bounce over the thumbtack-stippled bulletin board and slide lightly across the red

(*BREAK GLASS IN CASE OF EMERGENCY*)
fire-alarm box.

Miss Bird *liked* it. Miss Bird *liked* making him have a red face. In front of Cathy Scott—who *never* needed to go to the basement; was that fair?—and everybody else.

*Old b-i-t-c-h*, he thought. He spelled because he had decided last year that God didn't say it was a sin if you spelled.

He went into the boys' bathroom.

It was very cool inside, with a faint, not unpleasant smell of chlorine hanging pungently in the air. Now, in the middle of the morning, it was clean and deserted, peaceful and quite pleasant, not at all like the smoky, stinky cubicle at the Star Theater downtown.

The bathroom

(*!basement!*)
was built like an "L," the short side lined with tiny square mirrors and white porcelain washbowls and a paper towel dispenser;

(*NIBROC*)
the longer side with two urinals and three toilet cubicles.

Charles went around the corner after glancing morosely at his thin, rather pallid face in one of the mirrors.

The tiger was lying down at the far end, just underneath the pebbly-white window. It was a large tiger, with tawny venetian

26

blinds and dark stripes laid across its pelt. It looked up alertly at Charles, and its green eyes narrowed. A kind of silky, purring grunt issued from its mouth. Smooth muscles flexed, and the tiger got to its feet. Its tail switched, making little chinking sounds against the porcelain side of the last urinal.

The tiger looked quite hungry and very vicious.

Charles hurried back the way that he had come. The door seemed to take forever to wheeze pneumatically closed behind him, but when it did, he considered himself safe. This door only swung in, and he could not remember ever reading or hearing that tigers are smart enough to open doors.

Charles wiped the back of his hand across his nose. His heart was thumping so hard that he could hear it. He still needed to go to the basement, worse than ever.

He squirmed, winced, and pressed a hand against his belly. He *really* had to go to the basement. If he could only be sure that no one would come, he could use the girls'. It was right across the hall. Charles looked at it longingly, knowing that he would never dare, not in a million years. What if Cathy Scott should come? Or—black horror!—what if *Miss Bird* should come?

Perhaps he had imagined the tiger.

He opened the door wide enough for one eye and peeked in.

The tiger was peeking back from around the angle of the "L," its eye a sparkling green. Charles thought he could see a tiny blue fleck in that deep brilliance, as if the tiger's eye had eaten one of his own. As if—

A hand slid around his neck.

Charles gave a stifled cry and felt his heart and stomach cram up into his throat. For one terrible moment he thought that he was going to wet himself.

It was Kenny Griffen, smiling complacently. "Miss Bird sent me after you 'cause you been gone six years. You're in trouble."

"Yeah, but I can't go to the basement," Charles said, feeling faint with the fright that Kenny had given him.

"Yer constipated!" Kenny chortled gleefully. "Wait'll I tell *Caaathy!*"

"You better not!" Charles said urgently. "Besides, I'm not. There's a tiger in there."

"What's he doing?" Kenny asked. "Takin' a leak?"

"I don't know," Charles said, turning his face to the wall. "I just wish he'd go away." He began to weep.

"Hey," Kenny said, bewildered and a little frightened. "Hey."

"What if I *have* to go? What if I can't help it? Miss Bird'll say—"

"Come on," Kenny said, grabbing his arm in one hand and pushing the door open with the other. "You're making it up."

They were inside before Charles, terrified, could break free and cower against the door.

"Tiger," Kenny said disgustedly. "Boy, Miss Bird's gonna kill you."

"It's around the other side."

Kenny began to walk past the washbowls. "Kitty, kitty, kitty? Kitty?"

"Don't!" Charles hissed.

Kenny disappeared around the corner. "Kitty, kitty? Kitty, kitty? Kit—"

Charles darted out the door again and pressed himself against the wall, waiting, his hands over his mouth and his eyes squinched shut, waiting, waiting for the scream.

There was no scream.

He had no idea how long he stood there, frozen, his bladder bursting. He looked at the door to the boys' bathroom. It told him nothing. It was just a door.

He wouldn't.

He *couldn't*.

But at last he went in.

The washbowls and the mirrors were neat, and the faint smell of chlorine was unchanged. But there seemed to be a smell underneath it. A faint, unpleasant smell, like freshly sheared copper.

With groaning (but silent) trepidation, he went to the corner of the "L" and peeped around.

The tiger was sprawled on the floor, licking its large paws with a long pink tongue. It looked incuriously at Charles. There was a torn piece of shirt caught in one set of claws.

But his need was a white agony now, and he couldn't help it. He *had* to. Charles tiptoed back to the white porcelain basin closest to the door.

Miss Bird slammed in just as he was zipping his pants.

"Why, you dirty, filthy little boy," she said almost reflectively.

Charles was keeping a weather eye on the corner. "I'm sorry,

Miss Bird . . . the tiger . . . I'm going to clean the sink . . . I'll use soap . . . I swear I will . . ."

"Where's Kenneth?" Miss Bird asked calmly.

"I don't know."

"Is he back there?"

"*No!*" Charles cried.

Miss Bird stalked to the place where the room bent. "Come here, Kenneth. Right this moment."

"Miss Bird—"

But Miss Bird was already around the corner. She meant to pounce. Charles thought that Miss Bird was about to find out what pouncing was really all about.

He went out the door again. He got a drink at the drinking fountain. He looked at the American flag hanging over the entrance to the gym. He looked at the bulletin board. Woodsy Owl said, GIVE A HOOT, DON'T POLLUTE. Officer Friendly said, NEVER RIDE WITH STRANGERS. Charles read everything twice.

Then he went back to the classroom, walked down his row to his seat with his eyes on the floor, and slid into his chair. It was a quarter to 11. He took out *Roads to Everywhere* and began to read about Bill at the rodeo.

# THE ROOM IN THE TOWER

### E. F. BENSON

IT WAS WHEN I was around 16 that a certain dream first came to me, and this is how it befell. It opened with my being set down at the door of a big red-brick house, where, I understood, I was going to stay. The servant who opened the door told me that tea was going on in the garden and led me through a low, dark-paneled hall, with a large open fireplace, on to a cheerful green lawn set around with flower beds. There were grouped around the tea table a small party of people, but they were all strangers to me except one, who was a schoolfellow named Jack Stone, clearly the son of the house, and he introduced me to his mother and father and a couple of sisters. I was, I remember, somewhat astonished to find myself here, for the boy in question was scarcely known to me, and I rather disliked what I knew of him: moreover, he had left school almost a year before. The afternoon was very hot, and an intolerable oppression reigned. On the far side of the lawn ran a red-brick wall, with an iron gate in its center, outside which stood a walnut tree. We sat in the shadow of the house opposite a row of long windows, inside which I could see a table with a cloth laid, glimmering with glass and silver. This garden front of the house was very long, and at one end of it stood a tower of three stories, which looked to me much older than the rest of the building.

Before long, Mrs. Stone, who, like the rest of the party, had sat in absolute silence, said to me, "Jack will show you your room; I have given you the room in the tower."

Quite inexplicably, my heart sank at her words. I felt as if I had known that I should have the room in the tower and that it contained something dreadful and significant. Jack instantly got up, and I understood that I had to follow him. In silence we passed through the hall and mounted a great oak staircase with many corners and arrived at a small landing with two doors set in it. He pushed one of these open for me to enter and, without coming in himself, closed it behind me. Then I knew that my conjecture had been right: there was something awful in the room, and with the terror of a nightmare growing swiftly and enveloping me, I awoke in a spasm of terror.

Now, that dream or variations on it occurred to me intermittently for 15 years. Most often it came in exactly this form—the arrival, the tea out on the lawn, the deadly silence succeeded by that one deadly sentence, the mounting with Jack Stone up to the room in the tower where horror dwelt—and it always came to a close in the nightmare of terror at that which was in the room, though I never saw what it was. At other times I experienced variations on this same theme. Occasionally, for instance, we would be sitting at dinner in the dining room, into the windows of which I had looked on the first night when the dream of this house visited me, but wherever we were, there was the same silence, the same sense of dreadful oppression and foreboding. And the silence I knew would always be broken by Mrs. Stone saying to me, "Jack will show you your room; I have given you the room in the tower." Upon which (this was invariable) I had to follow him up the oak staircase with many corners and enter the place that I dreaded more and more each time that I visited it in sleep. Or, again, I would find myself playing cards still in silence in a drawing room lit with immense chandeliers that gave a blinding illumination. What the game was I have no idea; what I remember, with a sense of miserable anticipation, was that soon Mrs. Stone would get up and say to me, "Jack will show you your room; I have given you the room in the tower." This drawing room where we played cards was next to the dining room and, as I have said, was always brilliantly illuminated, while the rest of the house was full of dusk and shadows. And yet, how often, in spite of those bouquets of lights, have I not pored over the cards that were dealt to me, scarcely able for some reason to see them. Their designs, too, were strange: there were no red suits, but all were black, and among them there were certain cards that were black all over. I hated and dreaded those.

As this dream continued to recur, I got to know the greater part of the house. There was a smoking room beyond the drawing room, at the end of a passage with a green baize door. It was always very dark there, and as often as I went there, I passed somebody whom I could not see in the doorway coming out.

Curious developments too took place in the characters that peopled the dream as might happen to living persons. Mrs. Stone, for instance, who, when I first saw her, had been black-haired, became gray, and instead of rising briskly, as she had done at first when she said, "Jack will show you your room; I have given you the room in the tower," got up very feebly, as if the strength was leaving her limbs. Jack also grew up and became a rather ill-looking young man with a brown mustache, while one of the sisters ceased to appear, and I understood that she was married.

Then it so happened that I was not visited by this dream for six months or more, and I began to hope, in such inexplicable dread did I hold it, that it had passed away for good. But one night after this interval I again found myself being shown out to the lawn for tea, and Mrs. Stone was not there, while the others were all dressed in black. At once I guessed the reason, and my heart leaped at the thought that perhaps this time I should not have to sleep in the room in the tower, and though we usually all sat in silence, on this occasion the sense of relief made me talk and laugh as I had never yet done. But even then matters were not altogether comfortable, for no one else spoke, but they all looked secretly at each other. And soon the foolish stream of my talk ran dry, and gradually an apprehension worse than anything I had previously known gained on me as the light slowly faded.

Suddenly a voice that I knew well broke the stillness, the voice of Mrs. Stone, saying, "Jack will show you your room; I have given you the room in the tower." It seemed to come from near the gate in the red-brick wall that bounded the lawn, and looking up, I saw that the grass outside was sown thick with gravestones. A curious grayish light shone from them, and I could read the lettering on the grave closest to me, and it said: "In evil memory of Julia Stone." And, as usual, Jack got up, and again I followed him through the hall and up the staircase with many corners. On this occasion it was darker than usual, and when I passed into the room in the tower, I could only just see the furniture, the position of which was already familiar to me. Also there was a dreadful odor of decay in the room, and I woke up screaming.

The dream, with such variations and developments as I have mentioned, went on at intervals for 15 years. Sometimes I would dream it two or three nights in succession; once, as I have said, there was an intermission of six months, but taking a reasonable average, I should say that I dreamed it quite as often as once in a month. It had, as is plain, something of a nightmare about it, since it always ended in the same appalling terror, which so far from getting less, seemed to me to gather fresh fear every time that I experienced it. There was too a strange and dreadful consistency about it. The characters in it, as I have mentioned, got regularly older, death and marriage visited this silent family, and I never in the dream, after Mrs. Stone had died, set eyes on her again. But it was always her voice that told me that the room in the tower was prepared for me, and whether we had tea out on the lawn or the scene was laid in one of the rooms overlooking it, I could always see her gravestone standing just outside the iron gate. It was the same too with the married daughter; usually she was not present, but once or twice she returned again, in company with a man, whom I took to be her husband. He, too, like the rest of them, was always silent. But, owing to the constant repetition of the dream, I had ceased to attach, in my waking hours, any significance to it. I never met Jack Stone again during all of those years, nor did I ever see a house that resembled this dark house of my dream. And then something happened.

I had been in London in this year, up till the end of July, and during the first week in August went down to stay with a friend in a house he had taken for the summer months, in the Ashdown Forest district of Sussex. I left London early, for John Clinton was to meet me at Forest Row station, and we were going to spend the day golfing and go to his house in the evening. He had his motorcar with him, and we set off, around five in the afternoon, after a thoroughly delightful day, for the drive, the distance being some ten miles. As it was still so early, we did not have tea at the clubhouse, but waited till we should get home. As we drove, the weather, which up till then had been, though hot, deliciously fresh, seemed to me to alter in quality and become very stagnant and oppressive, and I felt that indefinable sense of ominous apprehension that I am accustomed to before thunder. John, however, did not share my views, attributing my loss of lightness to the fact that I had lost both of my matches. Events proved, however, that I was right, though I do not think that the thunderstorm that broke that night was the sole cause of my depression.

Our way lay through deep, high-banked lanes, and before we had gone very far, I fell asleep and was only awakened by the stopping of the motor. And with a sudden thrill, partly of fear but chiefly of curiosity, I found myself standing in the doorway of the house of my dream. We went, I half wondering whether or not I was still dreaming, through a low, oak-paneled hall and out to the lawn, where tea was laid in the shadow of the house. It was set in flower beds, a red-brick wall, with a gate in it, bounded one side, and out beyond that was a space of rough grass with a walnut tree. The façade of the house was very long, and at one end stood a three-storied tower, markedly older than the rest.

Here for the moment all resemblance to the repeated dream ceased. There was no silent and somehow terrible family, but a large assembly of exceedingly cheerful persons, all of whom were known to me. And in spite of the horror with which the dream itself had always filled me, I felt nothing of it now that the scene of it was thus reproduced before me. But I felt the intensest curiosity as to what was going to happen.

Tea pursued its cheerful course, and before long Mrs. Clinton got up. And at that moment I think I knew what she was going to say. She spoke to me, and what she said was: "Jack will show you your room; I have given you the room in the tower."

At that, for half a second, the horror of the dream took hold of me again. But it quickly passed, and again I felt nothing more than the most intense curiosity. It was not very long before it was amply satisfied.

John turned to me.

"Right up at the top of the house," he said, "but I think you'll be comfortable. We're absolutely full. Would you like to go and see it now? By Jove, I believe that you are right and that we are going to have a thunderstorm. How dark it has become."

I got up and followed him. We passed through the hall and up the perfectly familiar staircase. Then he opened the door, and I went in. And at that moment sheer, unreasoning terror again possessed me. I did not know for certain what I feared; I simply feared. Then like a sudden recollection, when one remembers a name that has long escaped the memory, I knew what I feared. I feared Mrs. Stone, whose grave with the sinister inscription "In evil memory" I had so often seen in my dream, just beyond the lawn that lay below my window. And then once more the fear passed so completely that I wondered what there was to fear, and I found myself, sober and quiet and sane, in the room in the tower, the name of which I had so often heard in my dream and the scene of which was so familiar.

I looked around it with a certain sense of proprietorship and found that nothing had been changed from the dreaming nights in which I knew it so well. Just to the left of the door was the bed, lengthwise along the wall, with the head of it at an angle. In a line with it was the fireplace and a small bookcase; opposite the door, the outer wall was pierced by two lattice-paned windows, between which stood the dressing table, while ranged along the fourth wall was the washstand and a big cupboard.

My luggage had already been unpacked, for the furniture of dressing and undressing lay orderly on the washstand and toilet table, while my dinner clothes were spread out on the coverlet of the bed. And then, with a sudden start of unexplained dismay, I saw that there were two rather conspicuous objects that I had not seen before in my dreams: one a life-size oil painting of Mrs. Stone and the other a black-and-white sketch of Jack Stone, representing him as he had appeared to me only a week before in the last of the series of these repeated dreams, a rather secret- and evil-looking man of around 30. His picture hung between the windows, looking straight across the room to the other portrait, which hung at the side of the bed. At that I looked next, and as I looked, I felt once more the horror of a nightmare seize me.

It represented Mrs. Stone as I had seen her last in my dream: old and withered and white-haired. But in spite of the evident feebleness of body, a dreadful exuberance and vitality shone through the envelope of flesh, an exuberance wholly malign, a vitality that foamed and frothed with unimaginable evil. Evil beamed from the narrow, leering eyes; it laughed in the demonlike mouth. The whole face was instinct with some secret and appalling mirth; the hands, clasped together on the knee, seemed shaking with suppressed and nameless glee. Then I saw also that it was signed in the left-hand bottom corner, and wondering who the artist could be, I looked more closely and read the inscription: "Julia Stone by Julia Stone."

There came a tap at the door, and John Clinton entered.

"Got everything you want?" he asked.

"Rather more than I want," said I, pointing to the picture.

He laughed.

"Hard-featured old lady," he said. "By herself too, I remember.

Anyhow, she can't have flattered herself much."

"But don't you see?" said I. "It's scarcely a human face at all. It's the face of some witch, of some devil."

He looked at it more closely.

"Yes; it isn't very pleasant," he said. "Scarcely a bedside manner, eh? Yes; I can imagine getting a nightmare, if I went to sleep with that close by my bed. I'll have it taken down if you like."

"I really wish you would," I said.

He rang the bell, and with the help of a servant, we detached the picture and carried it out onto the landing and put it with its face to the wall.

"By Jove, the old lady is a weight," said John, mopping his forehead. "I wonder if she had something on her mind."

The extraordinary weight of the picture had struck me, too. I was about to reply, when I caught sight of my own hand. There was blood on it, in considerable quantities, covering the whole palm.

"I've cut myself somehow," said I.

John gave a little startled exclamation.

"Why, I have too," he said.

Simultaneously the footman took out his handkerchief and wiped his hand with it. I saw that there was also blood on his handkerchief.

John and I went back into the tower room and washed off the blood; but neither on his hand nor on mine was there the slightest trace of a scratch or cut. It seemed to me that, having ascertained this, we both, by a sort of tacit consent, did not allude to it again. Something in my case had dimly occurred to me that I did not wish to think about. It was but a conjecture, but I fancied that I knew the same thing had occurred to him.

The heat and oppression of the air, for the storm that we had expected was still undischarged, increased very much after dinner, and for some time most of the party, among whom were John Clinton and myself, sat outside on the path bounding the lawn, where we had had tea. The night was absolutely dark, and no twinkle of star or moon ray could penetrate the pall of clouds that overset the sky. By degrees our assembly thinned, the women went up to bed, men dispersed to the smoking or billiard rooms, and by 11 o'clock my host and I were the only two left. All the evening I thought that he had something on his mind, and as soon as we were alone, he spoke.

"The man who helped us with the picture had blood on his hand too, did you notice?" he said. "I asked him just now if he had cut himself, and he said he supposed he had, but that he could find no mark of it. Now, where did that blood come from?"

By dint of telling myself that I was not going to think about it, I had succeeded in not doing so, and I did not want, especially just at bedtime, to be reminded of it.

"I don't know," said I, "and I don't really care so long as the picture of Mrs. Julia Stone is not by my bed."

He got up.

"But it's odd," he said. "Ha! Now you'll see another odd thing."

A dog of his, an Irish terrier by breed, had come out of the house as we talked. The door behind us into the hall was open, and a bright oblong of light shone across the lawn to the iron gate that led to the rough grass outside, where the walnut tree stood. I saw that the dog had all of his hairs up, bristling with rage and fright; his lips were curled back from his teeth, as if he was ready to spring at something, and he was growling to himself. He took not the slightest notice of his master or me, but stiffly and tensely walked across the grass to the iron gate. There he stood for a moment, looking through the bars and still growling. Then all of a sudden his courage seemed to desert him; he gave one long howl and scuttled back to the house with a curious crouching sort of movement.

"He does that half a dozen times a day," said John. "He sees something that he both hates and fears."

I walked to the gate and looked over it. Something was moving on the grass outside, and soon a sound that I could not instantly identify came to my ears. Then I remembered what it was: it was the purring of a cat. I lit a match and saw the purrer, a big blue Persian, walking around and around in a little circle just outside the gate, stepping high and ecstatically, with tail carried aloft like a banner. Its eyes were bright and shining, and every now and then it put its head down and sniffed at the grass.

I laughed.

"The end of that mystery, I am afraid," I said. "Here's a large cat having Walpurgis Night all alone."

"Yes, that's Darius," said John. "He spends half the day and all night there. But that's not the end of the dog mystery, for Toby and he are the best of friends, but the beginning of the cat mystery. What's the cat doing there? And why is Darius pleased, while Toby is terror-stricken?"

At that moment I remembered the rather horrible details of my dreams when I saw through the gate, just where the cat was now, the white tombstone with the sinister inscription. But before I could answer, the rain began, as suddenly and heavily as if a tap had been turned on, and simultaneously the big cat squeezed through the bars of the gate and came leaping across the lawn to the house for shelter. Then it sat in the doorway, looking out eagerly into the dark. It spat and struck at John with its paw as he pushed it in order to close the door.

Somehow, with the portrait of Julia Stone in the passage outside, the room in the tower had absolutely no alarm for me, and as I went to bed, feeling very sleepy and heavy, I had nothing more than interest for the curious incident about our bleeding hands and the conduct of the cat and dog. The last thing I looked at before I put out my light was the square, empty space by my bed where the portrait had been. Here the paper was of its original full tint of dark red; over the rest of the walls, it had faded. Then I blew out my candle and instantly fell asleep.

My awakening was equally instantaneous, and I sat bolt upright in bed under the impression that some bright light had been flashed in my face, though it was now absolutely pitch-black. I knew exactly where I was, in the room that I had dreaded in my dreams, but no horror that I ever felt when asleep approached the fear that now invaded and froze my brain.

Immediately after, a peal of thunder crackled just above the house, but the probability that it was only a flash of lightning that awoke me gave no reassurance to my galloping heart. Something I knew was in the room with me, and instinctively I put out my right hand, which was closest to the wall, to keep it away. And my hand touched the edge of a picture frame hanging close to me.

I sprang out of bed, upsetting the small table that stood by it, and I heard my watch, candle, and matches clatter onto the floor. But for the moment there was no need of light, for a blinding flash leaped out of the clouds and showed me that by my bed again hung the picture of Mrs. Stone. And instantly the room went into blackness again. But in that flash I saw another thing also, namely a figure that leaned over the end of my bed, watching me. It was dressed in some close-clinging white garment, spotted and stained with mold, and the face was that of the portrait.

Overhead the thunder cracked and roared, and when it ceased and the deathly stillness succeeded, I heard the rustle of movement coming closer to me and, more horrible yet, perceived an odor of corruption and decay. And then a hand was laid on the side of my neck, and close beside my ear I heard quick-taken, eager breathing. Yet I knew that this thing, though it could be perceived by touch, by smell, by eye, and by ear, was still not of this earth, but something that had passed out of the body and had the power to make itself manifest. Then a voice, already familiar to me, spoke.

"I knew you would come to the room in the tower," it said.

"I have been long waiting for you. At last you have come. Tonight I shall feast; before long we will feast together."

And the quick breathing came closer to me; I could feel it on my neck.

At that the terror, which I think had paralyzed me for the moment, gave way to the wild instinct of self-preservation. I hit wildly with both arms, kicking out at the same moment, and heard a little animal squeal, and something soft dropped with a thud beside me. I took a couple of steps forward, almost tripping over whatever it was that lay there, and by the merest good luck found the handle of the door. In another second I ran out on the landing and had banged the door behind me. Almost at the same moment I heard a door open somewhere below, and John Clinton, candle in hand, came running upstairs.

"What is it?" he said. "I sleep just below you and heard a noise as if—good heavens, there's blood on your shoulder."

I stood there, so he told me afterward, swaying from side to side, as white as a sheet, with the mark on my shoulder as if a hand covered with blood had been laid there.

"It's in there," I said, pointing. "She, you know. The portrait is in there too, hanging up on the place that we took it from."

At that he laughed.

"My dear fellow, this is a mere nightmare," he said.

He pushed by me and opened the door, I standing there simply inert with terror, unable to stop him, unable to move.

"Phew! What an awful smell," he said.

Then there was silence; he had passed out of my sight behind the open door. The next moment he came out again, as white as myself, and instantly shut it.

"Yes, the portrait's there," he said, "and on the floor is a thing—a thing spotted with earth, like what they bury people in. Come away, quick, come away."

How I got downstairs I hardly know. An awful shuddering and nausea of the spirit rather than of the flesh had seized me, and more than once he had to place my feet upon the steps, while every now and then he cast glances of terror and apprehension up the stairs. But in time we came to his dressing room on the floor below, and there I told him what I have here described.

The sequel can be made short; indeed, some of my readers have perhaps already guessed what it was, if they remember that inexplicable affair of the churchyard in West Fawley, some eight years ago, where an attempt was made three times to bury the body of a certain woman who had committed suicide. On each occasion the coffin was found in the course of a few days again protruding from the ground. After the third attempt, in order that the thing should not be talked about, the body was buried elsewhere in unconsecrated ground. Where it was buried was just outside the iron gate of the garden belonging to the house where this woman had lived. She had committed suicide in a room at the top of the tower in that house. Her name was Julia Stone.

Subsequently the body was again secretly dug up, and the coffin was found to be full of blood.

# BEYOND LIES THE WUB

### PHILIP K. DICK

THEY HAD ALMOST finished with the loading. Outside stood the Optus, his arms folded, his face sunk in gloom. Captain Franco walked leisurely down the gangplank, grinning.

"What's the matter?" he said. "You're getting paid for all of this."

The Optus said nothing. He turned away, collecting his robes. The Captain put his boots on the hem of the robe.

"Just a minute. Don't go off. I'm not finished."

"Oh?" The Optus turned with dignity. "I am going back to the village." He looked toward the animals and birds being driven up the gangplank into the spaceship. "I must organize new hunts."

Franco lit a cigarette. "Why not? You people can go out into the veldt and track it all down again. But when we run out halfway between Mars and Earth—"

The Optus went off, wordless. Franco joined the first mate at the bottom of the gangplank.

"How's it coming?" he said. He looked at his watch. "We've got a good bargain here."

The mate glanced at him sourly. "How do you explain that?"

"What's the matter with you? We need it more than they do."

"I'll see you later, Captain." The mate threaded his way up the plank, between the long-legged Martian go-birds, into the ship. Franco watched him disappear. He was just starting up after him, up the plank toward the port, when he saw *it*.

"My God!" He stood staring, his hands on his hips. Peterson was walking along the path, his face red, leading *it* by a string.

"I'm sorry, Captain," he said, tugging on the string. Franco walked toward him.

"What is it?"

The wub stood sagging, its great body settling slowly. It was sitting down, its eyes half shut. A few flies buzzed around its flank, and it swished its tail.

It sat. There was silence.

"It's a wub," Peterson said. "I got it from a native for fifty cents. He said that it was a very unusual animal. Very respected."

"This?" Franco poked the great sloping side of the wub. "It's a pig! A huge, dirty pig!"

"Yes, sir, it's a pig. The natives call it a wub."

"A huge pig. It must weigh four hundred pounds." Franco grabbed a tuft of the rough hair. The wub gasped. Its eyes opened, small and moist. Then its great mouth twitched.

A tear rolled down the wub's cheek and splashed onto the floor.

"Maybe it's good to eat," Peterson said nervously.

"We'll soon find out," Franco said.

★★★

The wub survived the takeoff, sound asleep in the hold of the ship. When they were out in space and everything was running smoothly, Captain Franco bade his men to fetch the wub from upstairs so that he might perceive what manner of beast it was.

The wub grunted and wheezed, squeezing up the passageway.

"Come on," Jones grated, pulling on the rope. The wub twisted, rubbing its skin off on the smooth chrome walls. It burst into the anteroom, tumbling down in a heap. The men leaped up.

"Good Lord," French said. "What is it?"

"Peterson says it's a wub," Jones said. "It belongs to him." He kicked at the wub. The wub stood up unsteadily, panting.

"What's the matter with it?" French came over. "Is it going to be sick?"

They watched. The wub rolled its eyes mournfully. It gazed around at the men.

"I think it's thirsty," Peterson said. He went to get some water. French shook his head.

"No wonder we had so much trouble taking off. I had to reset all of my ballast calculations."

Peterson came back with the water. The wub began to lap gratefully, splashing the men.

Captain Franco appeared at the door.

"Let's have a look at it." He advanced, squinting critically. "You got this for fifty cents?"

"Yes, sir," Peterson said. "It eats almost anything. I fed it on grain, and it liked that. And then potatoes, and mash, and scraps from the table, and milk. It seems to enjoy eating. After it eats, it lies down and goes to sleep."

"I see," Captain Franco said. "Now, as to its taste. That's the real question. I doubt if there's much point in fattening it up any more. It seems fat enough to me already. Where's the cook? I want him here. I want to find out—"

The wub stopped lapping and looked up at the Captain.

"Really, Captain," the wub said, "I suggest we talk of other matters."

The room was silent.

"What was that?" Franco said. "Just now."

"The wub, sir," Peterson said. "It spoke."

They all looked at the wub.

"What did it say? What did it say?"

"It suggested we talk about other things."

Franco walked toward the wub. He went all around it, examining it from every side. Then he came back over and stood with the men.

"I wonder if there's a native inside it," he said thoughtfully. "Maybe we should open it up and have a look."

"Oh, goodness!" the wub cried. "Is that all you people can think of, killing and cutting?"

Franco clenched his fists. "Come out of there! Whoever you are, come out!"

Nothing stirred. The men stood together, their faces blank, staring at the wub. The wub swished its tail. It belched suddenly.

"I beg your pardon," the wub said.

"I don't think there's anyone in there," Jones said in a low voice. They all looked at each other.

The cook came in.

"You wanted me, Captain?" he said. "What's this thing?"

"This is a wub," Franco said. "It's to be eaten. Will you measure it and figure out—"

"I think we should have a talk," the wub said. "I'd like to discuss this with you, Captain, if I might. I can see that you and I do not agree on some basic issues."

The Captain took a long time to answer. The wub waited good-naturedly, licking the water from its jowls.

"Come into my office," the Captain said at last. He turned and walked out of the room. The wub rose and padded after him. The men watched it go out. They heard it climbing the stairs.

"I wonder what the outcome will be," the cook said. "Well, I'll be in the kitchen. Let me know as soon as you hear."

"Sure," Jones said. "Sure."

The wub eased itself down in the corner with a sigh. "You must forgive me," it said. "I'm afraid that I'm addicted to various forms of relaxation. When one is as large as I—"

The Captain nodded impatiently. He sat down at his desk and folded his hands.

"All right," he said. "Let's get started. You're a wub? Is that correct?"

The wub shrugged. "I suppose so. That's what they call us, the natives, I mean. We have our own term."

"And you speak English? You've been in contact with Earth men before?"

"No."

"Then how do you do it?"

"Speak English? Am I speaking English? I'm not conscious of speaking anything in particular. I examined your mind—"

"My mind?"

"I studied the contents, especially the semantic warehouse, as I refer to it—"

"I see," the Captain said. "Telepathy. Of course."

"We are a very old race," the wub said. "Very old and very ponderous. It is difficult for us to move around. You can appreciate that anything so slow and heavy would be at the mercy of more agile forms of life. There was no use in us relying on physical defenses. How could we win? Too heavy to run, too soft to fight, too good-natured to hunt for game—"

"How do you live?"

"Plants. Vegetables. We can eat almost anything. We're very catholic. Tolerant, eclectic, catholic. We live and let live. That's how we've gotten along."

The wub eyed the Captain.

"And that's why I so violently objected to this business about having me boiled. I could see the image in your mind—most of me in the frozen food locker, some of me in the kettle, a bit for your pet cat—"

"So you read minds?" the Captain said. "How interesting.

Anything else? I mean, what else can you do along those lines?"

"A few odds and ends," the wub said absently, staring around the room. "A nice apartment you have here, Captain. You keep it quite neat. I respect life forms that are tidy. Some Martian birds are quite tidy. They throw things out of their nests and sweep them—"

"Indeed." The Captain nodded. "But to get back to the problem—"

"Quite so. You spoke of dining on me. The taste, I am told, is good. A little fatty, but tender. But how can any lasting contact be established between your people and mine if you resort to such barbaric attitudes? Eat me? Instead you should discuss questions with me, philosophy, the arts—"

The Captain stood up. "Philosophy. It might interest you to know that we will be hard put to find something to eat for the next month. An unfortunate spoilage—"

"I know." The wub nodded. "But wouldn't it be more in accord with your principles of democracy if we all drew straws or something along that line? After all, democracy is to protect the minority from just such infringements. Now, if each of us casts one vote—"

The Captain walked to the door.

"Nuts to you," he said. He opened the door. He opened his mouth.

He stood frozen, his mouth wide, his eyes staring, his fingers still on the knob.

The wub watched him. Presently it padded out of the room,

edging past the Captain. It went down the hall, deep in meditation.

The room was quiet.

"So you see," the wub said, "we have a common myth. Your mind contains many familiar myth symbols. Ishtar, Odysseus—"

Peterson sat silently, staring at the floor. He shifted in his chair.

"Go on," he said. "Please go on."

"I find in your Odysseus a figure common to the mythology of most self-conscious races. As I interpret it, Odysseus wanders as an individual aware of himself as such. This is the idea of separation, of separation from family and country. The process of individuation."

"But Odysseus returns to his home." Peterson looked out the port window, at the stars, endless stars, burning intensely in the empty universe. "Finally he goes home."

"As must all creatures. The moment of separation is a temporary period, a brief journey of the soul. It begins; it ends. The wanderer returns to land and race . . ."

The door opened. The wub stopped, turning its great head.

Captain Franco came into the room, the men behind him. They hesitated at the door.

"Are you all right?" French said.

"Do you mean me?" Peterson asked, surprised. "Why me?"

Franco lowered his gun. "Come over here," he said to Peterson. "Get up and come here."

There was silence.

"Go ahead," the wub said. "It doesn't matter."

Peterson stood up. "What for?"

"It's an order."

Peterson walked to the door. French caught his arm.

"What's going on?" Peterson wrenched loose. "What's the matter with you?"

Captain Franco moved toward the wub. The wub looked up from where it lay in the corner, pressed against the wall.

"It is interesting," the wub said, "that you are obsessed with the idea of eating me. I wonder why."

"Get up," Franco said.

"If you wish." The wub rose, grunting. "Be patient. It is difficult for me." It stood, gasping, its tongue lolling foolishly.

"Shoot it now," French said.

"For God's sake!" Peterson exclaimed. Jones turned to him quickly, his eyes gray with fear.

"You didn't see him—like a statue, standing there, his mouth open. If we hadn't come down, he'd still be there."

"Who? The Captain?" Peterson stared around. "But he's all right now."

They looked at the wub, standing in the middle of the room, its great chest rising and falling.

"Come on," Franco said. "Out of the way."

The men stepped aside toward the door.

"You are quite afraid, aren't you?" the wub said. "Have I done anything to you? I am against the idea of hurting. All I have done is try to protect myself. Can you expect me to rush eagerly to my death? I am a sensible being like yourselves. I was curious to see your ship, learn about you. I suggested to the native—"

The gun jerked.

"See," Franco said. "I thought so."

The wub settled down, panting. It put out its paw, pulling its tail around it.

"It is very warm," the wub said. "I understand that we are close to the jets. Atomic power. You have done many wonderful things with it—technically. Apparently your scientific hierarchy is not equipped to solve moral, ethical—"

Franco turned to the men, crowding behind him, wide-eyed, silent.

"I'll do it. You can watch."

French nodded. "Try to hit the brain. It's no good for eating. Don't hit the chest. If the rib cage shatters, we'll have to pick out the bones."

"Listen," Peterson said, licking his lips. "Has it done anything? What harm has it done? I'm asking you. And anyhow, it's still mine. You have no right to shoot it. It doesn't belong to you."

Franco raised his gun.

"I'm going out," Jones said, his face white and sick. "I don't want to see it."

"Me, too," French said. The men straggled out, murmuring. Peterson lingered at the door.

"It was talking to me about myths," he said. "It wouldn't hurt anyone."

He went outside.

Franco walked toward the wub. The wub looked up slowly. It swallowed.

"A very foolish thing," it said. "I am sorry that you want to do it. There was a parable that your Savior related—"

It stopped, staring at the gun.

"Can you look me in the eye and do it?" the wub said. "Can you do that?"

The Captain gazed down. "I can look you in the eye," he said. "Back on the farm we had hogs, dirty razorback hogs. I can do it."

Staring down at the wub, into the gleaming, moist eyes, he pressed the trigger.

The taste was excellent.

They sat glumly around the table, some of them hardly eating at all. The only one who seemed to be enjoying himself was Captain Franco.

"More?" he said, looking around. "More? And some wine, perhaps."

"Not me," French said. "I think I'll go back to the chart room."

"Me, too." Jones stood up, pushing back his chair. "I'll see you later."

The Captain watched them go. Some of the others excused themselves.

"What do you suppose the matter is?" the Captain said. He turned to Peterson. Peterson sat staring down at his plate, at the potatoes, the green peas, and at the thick slab of tender, warm meat.

He opened his mouth. No sound came.

The Captain put his hand on Peterson's shoulder.

"It is only organic matter now," he said. "The life essence is gone." He ate, spooning up the gravy with some bread. "I, myself, love to eat. It is one of the greatest things that a living creature can enjoy. Eating, resting, meditation, discussing things."

Peterson nodded. Two more men got up and went out. The Captain drank some water and sighed.

"Well," he said, "I must say that this was a very enjoyable meal. All of the reports I had heard were quite true—the taste of wub. Very fine. But I was prevented from enjoying this in times past."

He dabbed at his lips with his napkin and leaned back in his chair. Peterson stared dejectedly at the table.

The Captain watched him intently. He leaned over.

"Come, come," he said. "Cheer up! Let's discuss things."

He smiled.

"As I was saying before I was interrupted, the role of Odysseus in the myths—"

Peterson jerked up, staring.

"To go on," the Captain said. "Odysseus, as I understand him—"

# FEEDING THE DOG

## SUSAN PRICE

THIS STORY'S SUPPOSED to be true.

It's about a witch, one of the really bad kind, a man named Downing.

He'd spent years learning witchcraft, traveling all over the country to meet other witches and be taught by them. He married a witch's daughter, and they had a horde of children. They kept a pack of cats, too, who went out to steal for them, bringing back meat and fish from other people's tables. There were just as many children as there were cats, and some people said that the children were the cats; and the only people who doubted this were the people who thought that the children were worse than the cats. Downing and his wife cared just as much for all of them, and anybody who raised hand or stone against either children or cats had to spend the next few days in bed, aching all over, cursed by Witch Downing. And everybody knew that Witch Downing could do worse than make you ache. So, mostly, the little Downings, human and feline, got away with their thieving.

But a farmer named Hollis heard noises in his yard one night and came out to find three of Downing's children tormenting the pigs in his sty by hitting them with sticks. He shouted at them and told them to go away, and they threw stones at him and shouted names. Hollis was so angry then that he forgot about Witch Downing. The children were so used to getting away with everything that they didn't try to run away. Hollis got ahold of the eldest and gave him the first hiding that he'd ever had in his life. The other two ran away when they saw what was happening to their brother. They ran home and told their father.

Witch Downing went to see Farmer Hollis the next day and demanded money in compensation for the terrible injuries inflicted on his poor boy. Farmer Hollis was afraid of what he had done, but he wouldn't back down now, and he said, "What terrible injuries? I've done him no more harm than I've done my own sons—I've only given him the sore backside that he should have had a long time ago from you if you'd been any kind of a father! What favor do you think you're doing him, letting him grow up thinking that he can do whatever he pleases?"

"Don't preach at me!" Witch Downing said. He went home, thinking that no curse he'd ever set on anybody before was bad enough for Hollis.

So he made a thing. He killed a couple of his cats, and he caught a big dog, and he killed that, too. He used poisons and some of the worst magic he'd learned, and he made this thing that he called a dog—it looked something like a dog. But it was so black that you couldn't really see it, and its eyes shone all the time like a real dog's eyes do when light catches them—shone red, or green, and sometimes blue. It was big. At midnight Downing said to it, "Hollis." The thing went out, and it didn't come back that night. The next day Farmer Hollis was missing from his bed and couldn't be found anywhere.

Witch Downing boasted that he knew what had happened to Hollis and that people had better watch out! No one knew what he meant.

That night, Downing woke up and saw two bright green candle flames floating beside his bed. There was a shape around them, a blackness. Then the candle flames burned red, and teeth showed beneath them. It was the thing, the dog, come back. It sat beside Witch Downing's bed and looked at him. When he asked what it wanted, it made no movement or sound, but waited. When Downing tried to leave his bed, it growled, and he lay back quickly. He spoke incantations for dismissing spirits, but it stayed. At last he said, "Farmer Hollis's wife." Then the thing rose and went out.

People began to disappear. Farmer Hollis had vanished, and then his wife had disappeared the night after. The following day the vicar couldn't be found; and then a market woman vanished. On the fifth night, the disappearance was of a woman who'd chased the witch's cats away with pepper and, on the sixth night, Farmer Hollis's little son.

But Downing no longer boasted. Now he slunk around and jumped if a dog barked.

People who had nothing much to stay for began to leave the town, and Downing began to run out of names. Night after night the thing came, sat beside his bed, and waited. It was very patient. It waited and waited as Downing, all in a sweat, tried to think of a name that he hadn't given it before. Sometimes he kept it waiting almost until morning, and the closer morning came, the more excited the thing was. It panted like a real dog and stirred where it sat. Downing didn't want to find out what would happen if he kept the thing waiting until morning, and he would gabble out, "The boy who serves at the grocer's!" or "The girl in the green skirt who I pass in the lane!" And the thing would rise and go out.

Then came a night when Downing, as worn out as he was, must have dozed. He woke with a great shock and saw that the sky was turning pink! And the thing was pacing up and down by his bed, whining with excitement. "My wife!" Downing cried—and the thing leaped over him and onto his wife. There was a dreadful noise. Downing jumped from the bed and ran away. There was not an eyelash left of his wife when he returned.

But the thing came to his bedside that night; and he could think of no one. When the thing began to wave its tail, he said, "The baby." And there was no baby in his crib when Downing got up.

"My eldest son," he said, the next night; and on nights after that: "My eldest daughter—Billy—Anne—Mary . . . And when the last of his children had gone, the thing still came, sat beside him, fixed its eyes on him, and waited.

Downing had nothing to say. Toward dawn, the silence was

filled with the drumming of the thing's tail on the floorboards and a whine from its throat. The light increased—the thing couldn't stay any longer, and its master hadn't fed it. So it ate its master before it left—and who knows where it went or where it is now?

For all of Downing's learning, he had never learned that you can't dine with the Devil without becoming the meal.

# TEDDIES RULE, OKAY?

### NICHOLAS FISK

IF I COULD introduce you to Mandy and Tugsy, her teddy bear, you would see nothing surprising, nothing strange. A well-behaved little girl, you would think. Around six. Long, straight, yellow hair. Gray eyes that look at you without curiosity. Clean white socks, clean pink hands. So . . .

Aloud, you say, "How do you do, Mandy?" "How do you do?" she replies, politely and flatly. Then, "This is Tugsy." For a moment, as she holds out the teddy bear (but not close enough for you to touch it), her eyes seem to light up a little. But only a little. "How do you do, Tugsy?" you say.

"How do you do?" says the bear in a low, grumpy voice. It does not really speak, of course. Mandy supplies the voice. Some little children do this sort of thing imaginatively and well. Mandy does not. The bear's voice is not convincing.

Now Mandy's mother, Karen, enters the cool, long, disciplined, modern living room. She touches a switch in passing. Dove-gray curtains hiss gently, parting to reveal big frameless windows looking out on the enormous yard. "So you've met Amanda," says the mother, giving you a hygienic smile (you note that Mandy is

"Amanda" to her mother). "Do sit down. Such a glorious day, yet this morning it was quite chilly. . ." She smiles; you smile. She touches a button. A cart with tea things emerges from a wall. "I'm sure you'd like some tea," Mandy's mother says with a smile. Her teeth are too good to be true, too good to be false.

You drink excellent tea from fine plain white cups. Outside, the regiments of flowers bow obediently and in unison to the breeze. "Tea, Amanda?"

"Tugsy says he doesn't want no tea."

"Doesn't want *any* tea, Amanda. Pass the sandwiches to our guest, dear."

But Mandy says, "Tugsy says we're going outside to play." She leaves the room.

"Amanda and her teddy bear . . . !" says the mother with a suitable light laugh. You smile back, feeling the first beginnings of an ache around your jaw caused by too much polite smiling.

Nothing surprising, nothing strange, has happened.

But perhaps there is something a little surprising about Tugsy. Why should Mandy be so content with such an ordinary and scruffy teddy bear? Just think of the toys this rich little girl could have! Game-playing machines, TV games, dolls that walk and talk, squawking robots that hobble across the carpet spitting harmless fire, remote-control motorcars, electronic toys—

"She just worships that teddy bear," Mandy's mother says with a smile. "Her father and some of the men made her the most fantastic toys . . . But, no, she must have her teddy."

You return her smile and think, *Some of the men—what men?* Of course: the technicians, the scientists, the international army of white-coated wizards producing silicon chips, microprocessors, microcircuits, micromechanisms—all of the tiny things making such vast differences to our world. These men are Mandy's father's men. For Mandy's father is Kern, Lucius Kern. Kern Developments Incorporated. Lucius Kern is one of the masters, the emperors, of all of our futures.

"He left New York this morning," says Karen Kern, "and he promised faithfully that he'd be home for dinner. But you know him. Once he's on his treadmill . . ." She smiles. You smile back.

Outside in the yard, Mandy plays—if that is the word. She sits, pale legs neatly crossed, on the shiny green seat of a huge, unswinging swing with high-tensile white ropes. Her head is down. She talks, ceaselessly, to her teddy bear.

Lucius Kern is as clean and cool as his wife and daughter. I am only a writer—not a rich person, not a person whose fingernails are manicured—yet Lucius Kern talks to me.

He talks to me for two reasons. First, I am his tenant. I occupy the Victorian lodge of his vast estate. Second, we are opposites. He commutes by Concorde: I pedal a bike. He is so rich that money doesn't matter to him: I am so poor that money matters all the time. The gulfs between us keep us at a convenient and proper distance: so we get along well.

Not long ago he flung himself over one of the gulfs and talked to me about something that concerned him personally.

He said, "That bear of hers . . ." and scratched the thin blond hair on his small, neat head.

I said, "Yes?"

"I think it is the only thing she loves." He flinched at having to say the word "love."

"Kids have to have a friend—something to love. The teddy bear is her friend, and she loves it."

"She doesn't love *me*. I'm not surprised. I am not a good father to that child. I hardly see her. I neglect her. But what can I do?" He stared anxiously at me through his modernistic steel-framed spectacles. "What *should* I do?"

"Try to find time for her, I suppose. Talk to her more."

"But she won't talk to me! If I ask her a question, a simple question, she answers through that darn bear. If I say, 'Shall we go for a walk?' or something like that, she replies, 'Tugsy doesn't want walking.' She looks at the bear, not at me. What should I do?"

"Have a beer," I said, throwing him a can. He caught it awkwardly. I wished that he would go back to his big house and leave me alone. There was nothing that I could say to help him. How could I tell him the truth—that, for all of his virtues, he is somehow a frozen person? Like his wife. And, for that matter, like his daughter.

I saw him again a week later. I was chopping firewood, for his house. He was smiling.

"I've thought of something to please Mandy," he said. "A surprise for her. Something that will really please her. To do with her teddy."

"Now you're talking!" I said and went on chopping.

"That's it!" he said and actually laughed out loud.

"What do you mean?"

"Talking! That's the surprise!"

He would not tell me any more. It was a secret, he said. I had never seen him look so pleased and excited—almost schoolboyish.

That afternoon, I delivered the firewood. I went to the big house and stood in the hall, waiting for Mrs. Kern to appear and tell me where she wanted the wood stacked. In that still, cool, open-plan house, sound travels well. I heard again what I had often heard before: Mandy, upstairs, talking to her bear. "Do listen," she was saying. "It's going to be a tea party. Special. And you'll pass the cakes around. Without dropping any. Don't forget."

The bear grunted.

"Don't say you won't," Mandy said sternly. "You must. And don't make that face."

The bear grunted.

"And you must eat properly and not stuff," she commanded.

It went on. I liked listening. I heard the rattle of dolls' cups and the bear grunting. Then Mrs. Kern appeared. She told me where she wanted the firewood put. I did as she asked and left.

Later, when it was dark, Lucius Kern's amazingly elegant Aston Martin Lagonda swished past my lodge house. I glimpsed him in the back seat. He was sitting forward. He waved to me and grinned. As I learned later, he had Mandy's surprise in his lap.

It was quite a surprise.

The surprise was in three small packages. Two were the size of apples and very complicated. The third was simple and even smaller—two flat magnets, one for each of the bear's "hands." With the magnets in place behind the velvet paw pads, Tugsy could "hold" metal objects—knives and forks, for instance—to "eat" with.

The complicated things went inside the bear's stomach. One was a tiny power pack, amplifier, and loudspeaker to provide Tugsy with a voice.

The final package was a brain. An electronic brain, complete with a memory store, logic and response systems, emotive coders, a 2,000-word vocabulary, and a speech synthesizer. There was also a frequency analyzer that let Tugsy respond only to Mandy's voice and no other. Lucius Kern had a thing like a fountain pen that enabled him to translate his voice frequencies into Mandy's and thus test the bear's performance.

That gadgetry represented several thousand hours of highly paid brainpower and several million dollars' worth of high technology.

That night, while Mandy slept, Lucius plied razorblade, needle, and thread to insert the technology inside Tugsy's stuffed belly. He was not very good as a teddy-bear surgeon. The needle pricked him; the razor nicked him—but, in the darkness, he smiled at his work.

★★★

It is easy to imagine what happened in the morning:

Mandy woke up. She said, "Come on, Tugsy, get up. Don't be lazy."

And the bear spoke! "Good morning," it said.

She said, "*What?*" and the bear repeated, "Good morning."

Perhaps Mandy's eyes and mouth opened wide in amazement. If they did, they were very soon brought under control. As she always did, she washed and dressed herself, without help, and went down to breakfast.

Lucius Kern was there, waiting. "Well, Mandy," he said, kissing her clean, cool face, "and how are you today?"

Not looking at her father, Mandy poured milk on her corn flakes and offered the box to Tugsy. The bear stared glassily ahead. Mandy said, "Tugsy doesn't want no corn flakes."

Lucius leaned forward eagerly. "Tell me, Mandy . . . how *is* Tugsy today?"

Again ignoring him, Mandy said, "You've got to eat, Tugsy." She held out a spoon to the bear. It leaped into his paw. The magnets held it.

"Look, Mandy!" said her father. "Look! He's holding it!"

Mandy merely said—to Tugsy, not her father—"Hold your spoon *properly*!" and adjusted the spoon to a more correct angle.

"Why, Mandy," said her father, "isn't Tugsy clever! Holding his spoon. Soon he might even be talking, don't you think?"

Silently, Mandy ignored her father. Silently, she ate her breakfast.

★★★

Nevertheless, she began to change. Now, I seemed to see a little red warning light within her cool gray eyes. A secret light. I tried to eavesdrop on her talk with Tugsy, but succeeded only twice.

The first time she was having a pretend quarrel with him.

I could hear her sharp, clear little voice, but could not make out the words spoken by Tugsy in the bass growl that the Kern technicians had given him. She was saying, "I'll spank you! Yes, I will! Like this, and this, and this!" Tugsy growled a reply. There was a silence.

Then Mandy's voice said, "That's not true! You mustn't say that!" More growling. Then (astonishing words in that childish voice), "Might is *not* right! It isn't! It isn't, it isn't, it isn't!"

The bear growled. A horrible growl, it was. A threat, a sneer, an insult . . .

The second time I overheard them talk, the quarrel was real. She was saying, "Don't! Or I'll tell Mommy! I will! I will tell her!" The bear's growlings answered her for a long time; then she started to cry, bitterly. "All right," she said, "I won't. I promise I won't."

Her crying upset me. But the bear's growl frightened me.

I spoke my fears to Lucius. He said, "I know. You don't have to tell me. It's a battle, a war, between them."

"But what's the war *about*?" I demanded.

Lucius kept his face turned from me as he answered. He said, "Today's machines are clever. You wouldn't believe how clever.

They tell you that you can't make a machine with a proper brain, a mind of its own, but some of my technicians would tell you different . . ."

"What is the war about?" I repeated.

"Power," he said. "Just power. Who's the boss."

"But that's ridiculous! Your people designed the machine, programmed it—"

"Oh, yes, oh, yes!" he said, bitterly. "My people gave it everything they've got! Everything!" He quieted down. "The trouble is," he said, "they could have given it too much."

"But it's still only a machine, a gadget—"

"Impatient," Lucius said. "It's getting impatient with Mandy. Impatient with her human weakness—her ignorance—her lack of logic. She's only a child, while he—it—is a very adult product . . . Don't you see? Its program is *better* than hers! Or yours, or mine! It thinks that it could manage things better than Mandy . . ."

"Better than anyone?" I suggested. "Better than me or you?"

Lucius stood up jerkily and said, "I'm getting rid of it. Taking it out. Chucking it out. Tonight."

Now we must imagine again. Lucius never talks about what happened. And Mandy—who can fathom Mandy?

This is the sequence of that night's events as I see them:

Lucius goes into his daughter's bedroom in the middle of the night. Very carefully, he removes the bear from the sleeping child's arms.

He produces a razorblade. He will use it to cut open the stomach.

Does the bear do anything? It is easy enough to imagine the round, button eyes staring at nothing in the dimness—and the cozy black nose and the sewn-in smile.

Does it say anything? Could it really have said the words that Lucius repeated, half dazed, nursing his injured hand, an hour or so later?

Did it really say, in that thick, deep, growl, *Better not! Better not!*?

Who knows? But, certainly, there is Lucius with the razorblade. He bends over the bear in the near darkness. He brings the blade to the almost invisible stitches—

And something goes wrong! The blade seems to be snatched from his fingers—attaches itself to the magnet under the bear's paw. Lucius gasps, flurries, reaches for the blade—and cuts his hand open from the ball of his thumb to the tip of his little finger. An appalling cut. A cut so bad that the blood gushes and spouts.

A cut so bad that you would think that there must have been a blow behind it.

Mandy awakes. "What are you doing, Daddy?"

"Nothing. I—a cut on my hand—bathroom—"

"Tugsy's got something sticky on him."

"In a minute—the bathroom—" He blunders to the bathroom, turns on the cold water, and watches his blood making a pink swirl in the basin. He watches it sickly and hears Mandy's prim and proper little voice: "You're dirty, Tugsy. Messy and sticky."

By the time that Lucius Kern has stopped the blood with a towel and cleaned up the pink-flecked washbasin, Mandy is asleep again.

Presumably the bear is asleep too—if that brain ever sleeps.

Lucius came to see me the next day. His hand was bandaged. "It didn't work," he said. "I failed." He looked awful. "What should I do?"

"Take the bear," I said. "Tear it from her arms if necessary. Then go down into the basement and *burn* the blasted thing."

"I couldn't do that . . ."

"You could. That great log fire of yours—I get the logs. You use plenty."

"I don't mean that—"

"I know you don't. I'll do it for you, if you like. I'll take the bear and burn it."

"It might—it might not *consent* to being destroyed . . ."

"Don't be ridiculous. Look, I know you've had a nasty experience, but—I'll do it. Now, immediately. Lead me to it."

I pushed his shoulders and made him walk to his house. We neared the house, and we both called, "Mandy!" We kept calling. We tried all of the places that she might be. There was no answer. We searched the yard and the house. My throat was dry.

We found her in the kitchen or, rather, the washroom—an underground, tiled, splendid private laundry room.

She was sitting on a chair with her nose almost touching the glass of a washing machine. The glass was a sort of porthole. You

could see the water swooshing around—and sometimes a
glimpse of tan material, sodden, behind the glass.

"Loop the loop," Mandy said. "Go on. That's right. Again."

"Mandy!" said Lucius.

But she silenced him. "He's flying, Tugsy is," she said.
"Learning to loop the loop. You can watch if you like. He was all
sticky with blood. Dirty blood." She sniffed disgustedly and
returned to watching Tugsy looping the loop in the washing
machine.

Behind her back, I pointed a finger at the porthole and
whispered to Lucius. "*Water . . . ?*" I drew my finger across my
throat.

"*It might,*" he whispered back.

Mandy hung Tugsy on the clothesline to dry.

It was a warm, sunny day. Two hours later he was completely
dry. I said to Lucius, "I've half a mind to get my shotgun and blow
a hole through the bear."

He replied, "Perhaps the water will have done it. It's delicate,
that circuitry . . ."

Lucius told me that he crept into her room that night, took
something that looked like a fountain pen from his pocket, and
spoke into it. "Tugsy! Can you hear me? Speak to me. Tugsy!
Speak to me!"

There was no reply. Tugsy's brain was dead.

Yet after all of this, and despite the slow-healing cut on his
throbbing hand, Lucius still felt guilty about "killing" Mandy's

bear. "It was her special surprise," he told me, "her treat. And now it's gone."

"Thank heaven for that."

"But I *owe* her a treat . . . I haven't been a good father to her . . . She must be terribly upset. Of course, she never says anything to me; she bottles things up—"

"She's good at bottling things up."

"If only I knew how she's *feeling*, what she's *thinking*."

Later he made his clumsy attempt to find out. I was cutting roses at the time, near the swing—a quiet, hidden job. I eavesdropped and heard his uneasy questions and her clear yet baffling answers.

"Mandy—no, listen to me, dear—Mandy, you love talking to Tugsy, don't you? You talk to him all the time, don't you?"

"Tugsy wants me to go and play," Mandy said pettishly, turning from Lucius. He caught her arm.

"No, wait, Mandy. You talk to Tugsy. Does Tugsy talk to *you*?"

Through my screen of roses, I saw Mandy's blank, sealed face. She eyed her father over the top of Tugsy's head. She said nothing.

"What I mean is . . . if he *used* to talk to you but *stopped* talking to you—I mean, if he suddenly seemed to give up talking—you wouldn't be too upset, would you?"

Mandy's face turned pink. Her lower lip stuck out. "He's always talking," she said. "He always did talk. He always will talk. He's talking to me now!"

"But, Mandy—" Lucius began. She pulled her arm free and

walked fast to the swing. She sat on it, Tugsy on her lap. Lucius watched her go. He had made a mess of things and knew it.

On the swing, Mandy and Tugsy had their heads together. The two of them seemed to be talking, talking, talking.

Lucius steeled himself and walked to the swing. He stood in front of her, demanding her attention. "Mandy!" he said. "Is Tugsy talking to you now?"

"I told you. Yes."

"All right. What's he talking about?"

She stared at him with eyes that seemed very big and cold and gray. *Doll's eyes*, I thought.

"What's he talking about?" her father insisted.

"He's talking about—*you*," Mandy answered. Her voice was clear and little-girlish and venomous. Her father flinched back from her words.

"Yes, *you*," Mandy said. She smiled and thrust her head forward. Tugsy's head went forward too. The sun lit Mandy's dolllike smile and filled the teddy bear's glassy, staring eyes with light.

It was so bright, the sun, that each and every stitch that formed the tight little smile of Tugsy's curling black lips seemed clear and distinct to me.

"All about you," Mandy said, singsonging the words now. "Making plans. Aren't we, Tugsy? Plans for Daddy. Oh, yes!"

She bounced up and down on the swing's seat, nodding her head and smiling.

Tugsy bounced on her lap, nodding his head and smiling too.

# GRENDEL THE MONSTER

## ELEANOR FARJEON

IT CAME INTO the mind of King Hrothgar that he would build a great hall in his kingdom of Denmark, a greater hall than any man had ever built before. And when it was built, he called it Heorot. High up in the air rose the roof of Heorot, and so strong were the walls that it seemed as though nothing but fire could ever destroy them.

Then King Hrothgar made a great banquet for his people, and to all who came he gave golden rings.

Now, outside the hall in the dark forest lived a dreadful monster named Grendel, a creature who was part man and part beast. The sound of the laughter in Heorot made him wild, and he hated the song of the minstrel. So when night fell, he crept to the hall, and there he saw Hrothgar's men sleeping after the feast. Right away Grendel seized 30 of the sleepers and fled yelling back to his forest, where he devoured them.

The next morning there was weeping and wailing in Heorot. And in the night the monster Grendel came again and devoured even more of those who slept there. For 12 years he continued to come by night to the hall of Hrothgar and to the houses of all of his friends, doing them dreadful harm. The tale of it went into distant lands and came at last to the ears of Hygelac, the king of the Goths, and of Beowulf, his young kinsman.

Now, Beowulf was a great hero, and he had the strength of 30 men.

So he ordered a swift boat to be prepared and took 14 of his friends with him to help him rid Hrothgar of Grendel the monster. Over the foamy sea went the ship like a bird and at last came in sight of a land of shining cliffs and towering hills and headlands running out into the waves. Eagerly, Beowulf landed with his 14 Goths, and they ran down the hill till they came to the glorious hall, of which they had often heard. For no king in the world had so famous a hall as Heorot. At the door of the hall stood King Hrothgar's herald, who said, "Whence come you, you tall, bold fellows, with your shields and helmets and spears? And who are you?"

"My name is Beowulf," said he. "Take me to your king, and I will tell him why I come."

Then Beowulf was taken in to Hrothgar, and the hero said to the king, "Hail, Hrothgar! I am kinsman to Hygelac, the king of the Goths, and young as I am, I have undertaken many deeds and seen much danger. And now I am come to fight the monster Grendel single-handed."

Then King Hrothgar rejoiced and answered, "Beowulf, my friend, tonight you shall keep guard in the hall where Grendel has done so many terrible things. But first sit down and share our feast with us."

A table was cleared for Beowulf and the Goths, and there they sat and drank beer with the Danes, and the men sang jovial songs together.

Then Hrothgar's queen came in in her gold array, bearing a great jeweled cup full of mead in her hands. She offered it in turn to all of the men, first to the king and last to Beowulf. While the hero drank, she spoke words of thanks and praise for his coming. And Beowulf said, "As I sat in my boat, I vowed to myself to free you from the monster or die in the struggle."

The words of the hero made the queen glad. Then in her gold array she went and sat by the king.

The feast came to an end, the king and queen departed with the Danes, and Beowulf and the Goths lay down in the hall. But first Beowulf took off his armor, saying, "Since Grendel the monster fights only with his naked strength, so will I."

Soon the Goths, who should have guarded the hall, were sleeping—all but one. Beowulf waked and watched.

Then through the night came Grendel, tearing along in his fury to the hall to get his supper of men. The iron-barred doors sprang open at his touch, and there on the paved floor he saw the sleeping Goths. His fury turned to laughter at the sight, and before Beowulf could stop him, he had seized the closest sleeper and devoured him.

The next he came to was Beowulf himself. He reached out his great arm like a fang, but Beowulf gripped the arm before it could clutch him. At that mighty grip, Grendel knew that he had met the strongest man in the world.

Now the monster was full of fear and tried to get away. But Beowulf grappled with him and would not let him go. Up and down and to and fro raged Grendel, but he could not get free from Beowulf's grip. The hall was filled with roaring; the sides and roof shook with the struggles of the hero and the monster. The seats were torn up, the golden walls destroyed, and in the distance the Danes heard the great noise and trembled in their beds.

At last Grendel got his death wound. With a mighty tug, Beowulf pulled the arm clean out of the monster's shoulder. Grendel gave one last howl and fled back to his forest to die, and Beowulf fixed the arm in the roof of the hall as a sign that all danger from Grendel was past.

By the light of the morning came the king with his lords and the queen with her ladies along the path to the hall. When Hrothgar saw the arm in the roof, he said, "Beowulf, I will love you forever like my own son for the deeds you have done."

"I wish all the same," said Beowulf, "that you could have seen the monster himself. However, there is his arm."

Then men and women came and made Heorot new and lovely. They mended the wrecked walls and seats and hung the hall with golden cloths and pictures. And when all was ready, another great feast was held there, and the king gave Beowulf a banner, a helmet, and a coat of mail, all wrought with gold. His own rich and mighty sword he gave also to the hero. And to these gifts he added eight horses with cheek plates of gold, and on one of them was the gay silver saddle that was the king's own war saddle. And the queen gave Beowulf golden rings and armlets, and a golden mantle, and the grandest collar in the world, all set with jewels. All of Beowulf's companions were likewise given precious gifts. And Heorot was filled with the sound of music.

After the feast the Goths and Danes lay down and slept once more in the hall; but Beowulf slept in a special room that had been made ready for him. If he had only slept in Heorot that night, it might have saved much sorrow.

For outside in the dark forest lived an old hag, Grendel's mother, at the bottom of a dreary pool. And when Grendel the monster fled back to her and died, she was filled with rage. That night she came out of her pool and burst into the hall where the Danes and Goths were sleeping; and she fell on Beowulf's dearest friend, killed him, and fled away with his head.

In the morning when all was known, Beowulf cried to Hrothgar, "Rouse up, guardian of the kingdom! Your men and mine must follow the track of the hag, and whether she hides in the dark forest, in the depths of the earth, or at the bottom of the sea, she shall not escape me!"

So the Danes and Goths rode forth from Heorot and followed Beowulf into the forest; and after a long time they found the dreary pool, and there on the brink of it lay the head of Beowulf's friend. Then the men blew a blast on their horns and sat down by the pool. At the sound of the blast, strange creatures rose up in the water and swam around: sea snakes, and water serpents, and dragons. But they could not make the heart of

Beowulf afraid. He put on his armor, bade the men watch for him, and plunged into the pool.

For nine hours the men sat and watched, but Beowulf did not return. Then the Danes would wait no more, but went back sadly to Heorot to tell the king that Beowulf was dead. But the Goths, who were Beowulf's own men, still waited by the pool.

Now, when Beowulf leaped into the pool, he began to sink, and the hag, who was waiting for him, seized him and bore him to the bottom. The pool was so deep that it took them the best part of the day. There, Beowulf found himself in a strange hall, with a roof that kept off the water, and it was brightly lit with fire. The walls of the hall were hung with mighty weapons, and the floor was scattered with treasures. And farther on lay the dead body of Grendel the monster.

Now Beowulf and the hag began to fight, and Beowulf drew his great sword, which had never failed him yet. But strange to tell, the sword could not hurt the hag; when it touched her, the edge of it turned aside. It was the first time that Beowulf's sword had not served him. So he flung the sword away and grappled with the hag with his hands. First he flung her down, and then she rose up and flung him down; but her knife could not cut through his armor any more than his sword could cut through her skin.

Then Beowulf got on his feet again, and he saw among the weapons on the wall an old and monstrous cutlass, made for the use of giants. He snatched it from the wall and struck at the hag with it. Instantly she fell, and the fight was ended.

Now Beowulf made ready to return to the top of the pool;

but first he picked up his own sword again. He would not take any of the treasures from the hall; the only thing he took was the head of Grendel as a sign that the monster was really dead.

When he came swimming up through the pool, his Goths rejoiced to see him whole and sound. They put the head of Grendel on a pole, and it took four of them to bear it through the forest. And so they marched once more to Heorot with Beowulf in their midst. When they entered Heorot, where the king and queen sat among the Danes, all there were startled at the sight of the head, but were filled with joy because Beowulf was alive.

Then the king rose up and thanked and praised him, calling him his beloved Beowulf. And a new feast was made, and they drank till night grew dim above them and it was time to sleep again.

But when the voice of the raven was heard at sunrise, Beowulf rose and said that he must take ship again for his own country. And King Hrothgar clasped him, and kissed him, and wept; for the old king had come to love the young hero better than any other man.

So Beowulf, wearing his rich gifts of golden armor, went over the grass and down to the sea where his swift ship lay at anchor. And he and the Goths got into the ship and sailed away to their own land again.

# A GRAVE MISUNDERSTANDING

## LEON GARFIELD

I AM A dog. I think you ought to know right away. I don't want to save it up for later, because you might begin to wonder what sort of a person it was who went around on all fours, sniffing at bottoms and peeing up against lampposts in public streets. You wouldn't like it; and I don't suppose you'd care to have anything more to do with me.

The truth of the matter is, we have different standards—me and my colleagues, that is; not in everything, I hasten to bark, but in enough for it to be noticeable. For instance, although we are as fond of a good walk as the next person, love puppies and smoked salmon, we don't go in much for reading. We find it hard to turn the pages. But, on the other paw, a good, deep snout full of mingled air as it comes humming off a garbage dump can be as teasing to us as a sonnet. Indeed, there are rhymes in rancid odors such as you'd never dream of; and every puddle tells a story.

We see things too. Only the other day, when me and my Person were out walking and going as brisk as biscuits through that green and quiet place of marble trees and stony, lightless lampposts, where people bury their bones and never dig them up, I saw a ghost. I stopped. I glared, I growled, and my hair stood up on end—

"What the devil's the matter with you now?" demanded my Person.

"What a beautiful dog!" said the ghost, who knew that I knew what she was and that we both knew that my Person did not.

She was the lifeless, meaningless shell of a young female person whose bones lay not very far away. No heart beat within her, there was wind in her veins, and she smelled of worm crumble and pine.

"Thank you," said my Person with a foolishly desiring smile, for the ghost's eyes were very come-hitherish, even though her hither was thither, under the grass. "He is rather a handsome animal. Best of breed at Crufts, you know." The way to his heart was always open through praise of me.

"Does he bite?" asked the ghost, watching me with all of the empty care of nothingness trying to be something.

"SHE'S DEAD—SHE'S DEAD!"

"Stop barking!" said my Person. "Don't be frightened. He wouldn't hurt a fly. Do you come here often?"

"Every day," murmured the ghost, with a sly look toward her bones. She moved a little closer to my Person. A breeze sprang up, and I could smell it blowing right through her, like frozen flowers. "He looks very fierce," said the ghost. "Are you sure that he's kind?"

"COME AWAY—COME AWAY!"

"Stop barking!" commanded my Person, and he looked at the ghost with springtime in his eyes. If only he could have smelled the dust inside her head and heard the silence inside her breast! But it was no good. All he could see was a silken smile. He was only a person and blindly trusted his eyes ...

"Dogs," said the ghost, "should be kept on a leash in the churchyard. There's a notice on the gate." She knew that I knew where she was buried and that I'd just been going to dig up her bones.

My person obeyed; and the ghost looked at me as if to say, "Now you'll never be able to show him that I'm dead!"

"SHE'S COLD! SHE'S EMPTY! SHE'S GRANDDAUGHTER DEATH!"

"Stop barking!" shouted my Person and, dragging me after, walked on, already half in love with the loveless ghost.

We passed very close to her bones. I could smell them, and I could hear the little nibblers dryly rustling. I pulled, I strained, I jerked to dig up her secret ...

"He looks so wild!" said the ghost. "His eyes are rolling, and his jaws are dripping. Are you sure that he doesn't have a fever? Don't you think he ought to go to the vet?"

"He only wants to run off and play," said my Person. "Do you live near here?"

"YES! YES! RIGHT BY THAT MARBLE LAMPPOST! SIX PAWS DEEP IN THE EARTH!"

"Stop barking!" said my Person. "Do you want to wake up the

dead?"

The ghost started. Then she laughed, like the wind among rotting leaves. "I have a room nearby," she murmured. "A little room all to myself. It is very convenient, you know."

"A little room all to yourself?" repeated my Person, his heart beating with eager concern. "How lonely that must be!"

"Yes," she said. "Sometimes it is very lonely in my little room, even though I hear people walking and talking upstairs, over my head."

"Then let me walk back with you," said my Person, "and keep you company!"

"No dogs allowed," said the ghost. "They would turn me out, you know."

"Then come my way!" said my Person; and the ghost raised her imitation eyebrows in imitation surprise. "Madam, will you walk?" sang my Person laughingly. "Madam, will you talk? Madam, will you walk and talk with me?"

"I don't see why not," the ghost said with a smile.

"BECAUSE SHE'S DEAD—DEAD—DEAD!"

"Stop barking!" said my Person. "'I will give you the keys of heaven; I will give you the keys of my heart . . .'"

"The keys of heaven?" The ghost sighed. "Would you really?"

"And the keys of my heart! Will you have dinner with me?"

"Are you inviting me into your home?"

"NO GHOSTS ALLOWED! SHE'LL TURN ME OUT!"

"Stop barking! Yes . . . if you'd like to!"

"Oh, I would indeed—I would indeed!"

"DON'T DO IT! YOU'LL BE BRINGING DEATH INSIDE OUR HOME!"

"For God's sake, stop that barking! This way . . . this way . . ."

It was hopeless, hopeless! There was only one thing left for a dog to do. She *knew* what it was, of course: she could see it in my eyes. She walked on the other side of my Person and always kept him between herself and me. I bided my time . . .

"Do you like Italian food?" asked my Person.

"No spaghetti," murmured the ghost. "It reminds me of worms."

It was then that I broke free. I jerked forward with all of my strength and wrenched the leash out of my Person's grasp. He shouted! The ghost glared and shrank away. For a moment I stared into her eyes, and she stared into mine.

"Dogs must be kept on a leash!" whispered the ghost as I jumped. "There's a notice on . . . on . . . on . . ."

It was like jumping through cobwebs and feathers; and when I turned, she'd vanished like a puff of air. I saw the grass shiver, and I knew that she'd gone back to her bones.

"SHE WAS DEAD! SHE WAS DEAD! I TOLD YOU SO!"

My Person didn't answer. He was shaking, and he was trembling; for the very first time, he couldn't believe his eyes.

"What happened? Where—where is she? Where has she gone?"

I showed him. Trailing my leash, I went to where she lay, six paws under, and began to dig.

"No! No!" he shrieked. "For God's sake, let her lie there in peace!"

Thankfully, I stopped. The earth under the grass was thick and heavy, and the going was hard. I went back to my Person. He had collapsed on a bench and was holding his head in his hands. I tried to comfort him by licking his ear.

A female person walked neatly by. She was young and smooth and shining and smelled of coffee and cats. She was dressed in the softest of white.

"Oh, what a beautiful dog," she said, pausing to admire me.

He stared up at her. His eyes widened; his teeth began to chatter. He could not speak.

"GO ON! GO ON! 'BEST OF BREED AT CRUFTS!' "

"Hush!" said the female person, reproaching me with a gentle smile. "You'll wake up the dead!"

"Is she real?" whispered my Person, his eyes as wide and round as cans. "Or is she a ghost? Show me, show me! Try to jump through her like you did before! Jump, jump!"

"BUT SHE'S REAL! SHE'S ALIVE!"

"Stop barking and jump!"

So I jumped. She screamed—but not in fright. She screamed with rage. My paws were still thick and filthy with churchyard mud and, in a moment, so was her dress.

"You—you madman!" she shouted at my shamefaced Person. "You told him to do it! You told him to jump! You're not fit to have a dog!"

"But—but—" he cried out as she stormed away, to report him, she promised, to the churchyard authorities and the SPCA.

"I TOLD YOU SHE WAS ALIVE! I TOLD YOU SO!"

"Stop barking!" wept my Person. "Please!"

# CAPTAIN MURDERER

## CHARLES DICKENS
From *THE UNCOMMERCIAL TRAVELER*

THE FIRST DIABOLICAL character who intruded himself on my peaceful youth (as I called to mind that day in Dullborough) was a certain Captain Murderer. This wretch must have been an offshoot of the Bluebeard family, but I had no suspicion of the consanguinity in those times. His warning name would seem to have awakened no general prejudice against him, for he was admitted into the best society and possessed immense wealth. Captain Murderer's mission was matrimony and the gratification of a cannibal appetite with tender brides. On his marriage morning, he always caused both sides of the way to church to be planted with curious flowers; and when his bride said, "Dear Captain Murderer, I never saw flowers like these before; what are they called?" he answered, "They are called garnish for house lamb," and laughed at his ferocious practical joke in a horrid manner, disquieting the minds of the noble bridal company with a very sharp show of teeth, then displayed for the first time. He made love in a coach and six and married in a coach and 12, and all of his horses were milk-white horses with one red spot on the back, which he caused to be hidden by the harness. For the spot *would* come there, though every horse was milk-white when Captain Murderer bought it. And the spot was young bride's blood. (To this terrific point I am indebted for my first personal experience of a shudder and cold beads on the forehead.) When Captain Murderer had made an end of feasting and revelry, and had dismissed the noble guests, and was alone with his wife on the day month after their marriage, it was his whimsical custom to produce a golden rolling pin and a silver pie board. Now, there was this special feature in the Captain's courtships that he always asked if the young lady could make pie crust; and, if she couldn't by nature or education, she was taught. Well! When the bride saw Captain Murderer produce the golden rolling pin and silver pie board, she remembered this and turned up her laced-silk sleeves to make a pie. The Captain brought out a silver pie dish of immense capacity, and the Captain brought out flour and butter and eggs and all things needful, except the inside of the pie; of materials for the staple of the pie itself, the Captain brought out none. Then said the lovely bride, "Dear Captain Murderer, what pie is this to be?" He replied, "A meat pie." Then said the lovely bride, "Dear Captain Murderer, I see no meat." The Captain humorously retorted, "Look in the glass." She looked in the glass, but still she saw no meat, and then the Captain roared with laughter and, suddenly frowning and drawing his sword, bade her roll out the crust. So she rolled out the crust, dropping large tears upon it all the time because he was so cross, and when she had lined the dish with crust and had cut the crust all ready to fit the top, the Captain called out, "I see the meat in the glass!"

And the bride looked up at the glass, just in time to see the Captain cutting off her head; and he chopped her in pieces, and peppered her, and salted her, and put her in the pie, and sent it to the baker's, and ate it all, and picked the bones.

Captain Murderer went on in this way, prospering exceedingly, until he came to choose a bride from two twin sisters and at first didn't know which to choose. For, though one was fair and the other dark, they were both equally beautiful. But the fair twin loved him, and the dark twin hated him, so he chose the fair one. The dark twin would have prevented the marriage if she could, but she couldn't; however, on the night before it, much suspecting Captain Murderer, she stole out and climbed his garden wall, and looked in at his window through a chink in the shutter, and saw him having his teeth filed sharp. The next day she listened all day and heard him make his joke about the house lamb. And that day month he had the paste rolled out, and cut the fair twin's head off, and chopped her in pieces, and peppered her, and salted her, and put her in the pie, and sent it to the baker's, and ate it all, and picked the bones.

Now, the dark twin had had her suspicions much increased by the filing of the Captain's teeth and again by the house lamb joke. Putting all things together when he gave out that her sister was dead, she divined the truth and determined to be revenged. So, she went up to Captain Murderer's house, and knocked the knocker, and pulled at the bell, and, when the Captain came to the door, said, "Dear Captain Murderer, marry me next, for I always loved you and was jealous of my sister." The Captain took it as a compliment and made a polite answer, and the marriage was quickly arranged. On the night before it, the bride again climbed to his window and again saw him having his teeth filed sharp. At this sight she laughed, such a terrible laugh at the chink in the shutter that the Captain's blood curdled, and he said, "I hope nothing has disagreed with me!" At that, she laughed again, a still more terrible laugh, and the shutter was opened and a search made, but she was nimbly gone, and there was no one. The next day they went to church in a coach and 12 and were married. And that day month she rolled out the pie crust, and Captain Murderer cut off her head, and chopped her in pieces, and peppered her, and salted her, and put her in the pie, and sent it to the baker's, and ate it all, and picked the bones.

But, before she began to roll out the paste, she had taken a deadly poison of most awful character, distilled from toads' eyes and spiders' knees; and Captain Murderer had hardly picked her last bone, when he began to swell, and to turn blue, and to be all over in spots, and to scream. And he went on swelling and turning bluer, and being more all over in spots and screaming, until he reached from floor to ceiling and from wall to wall; and then, at one o'clock in the morning, he blew up with a loud explosion. At the sound of it, all of the milk-white horses in the stables broke their halters and went mad, and then they galloped over everybody in Captain Murderer's house (beginning with the family blacksmith who had filed his teeth) until all were dead, and then they galloped away.

Hundreds of times did I hear this legend of Captain Murderer in my early youth and added hundreds of times was there a mental compulsion upon me, in bed, to peep in at his window as the dark twin peeped, and to revisit his horrible house, and to look at him in his blue and spotty and screaming stage, as he reached from floor to ceiling and from wall to wall. The young woman who brought me acquainted with Captain Murderer had a fiendish enjoyment of my terrors and used to begin, I remember—as a sort of introductory overture—by clawing the air with both hands and uttering a long, low, hollow groan. So acutely did I suffer from this ceremony in combination with this infernal Captain that I sometimes used to plead that I thought I was hardly strong enough and old enough to hear the story again just yet. But, she never spared me one word of it and, indeed, commended the awful chalice to my lips as the only preservative known to science against "The Black Cat"—a weird and glaring-eyed supernatural tom, who was reputed to prowl around the world by night, sucking the breath of infancy, and who was endowed with a special thirst (as I was given to understand) for mine.

# SOMETHING

JOAN AIKEN

WHEN THE THING happened for the first time, I was digging up wild lilies to plant in my own little garden. Digging up wild lilies. A happy task. They are dark orange and grow down by the narrow, shallow brook that freezes solid in the winter. On that day it was babbling and murmuring placidly, and I sang a song, which I made up as I went along, to keep company with its murmur. "Wild lilies I find, wild lilies I bring, wild lilies, wild lilies, to flower in the spring." Overhead the alder trees arched, and the water birds, becoming used to my harmless presence, called their short, gargling answers. Once or twice a kingfisher flashed. There were trout in the water, but only tiny ones; I could feel them brush against my bare legs every now and then as I waded knee-deep along the course of the brook, which made an easier route than the tangled banks.

At the end of a whole afternoon spent in this manner my mind felt bare, washed clean, like the stones in the brook.

And then—suddenly: fear. Where did it come from? I had no means of knowing. *Menace.* Cold fear was all around me—in the dark arch of the trees, the tunnel they made (into which the stream vanished), the sharp croak of birds, the icy grip of the water on my calves, the gritty scour of the mud on my grimed and scraped hands. But, most of all, in my own mind, as if, down at the back of it, stood something hidden, watchful, *waiting*. In another minute I would see it and know what it was. In another minute I would go mad from terror.

Frenzied with haste to be away from there, I scrambled up the bank, snatching my trowel and the wooden bucket in which I had been putting my lily roots—dropping half of them; panic-stricken, never looking back, I thrust and battered a track through alders and brambles, tearing my shirt, scratching my arms and face. Mother would be furious, but I never gave that a thought. All my need was to get home—home—home to Grandfather's comforting presence.

Barefoot I ran over the plowed field, stubbing my toes on flints, reckless of sharp stubble ends and dry thistles with their lancing spines. Tonight I would need to spend hours squeezing them out, painfully one by one. Tonight was not now. Now if I did not find Grandfather, I would die of fear.

Luckily he was always to be found in the same place: placid on a backless chair with his dog, Flag, beside him, outside the smithy where my uncles Josef and Willi clanked on the anvil and roared on the bellows. A great gray carthorse waited patiently, one hoof tipped forward. A cone of fire burned bright in the dim forge, and there was Uncle Josef in his black leather apron, holding the gold and blazing shoe in his long tongs. For once I didn't wait and watch. I ran and clung tight to Grandfather. He felt frail and bony and smelled, as always, of straw and old man's odor and sweet tobacco.

"Grandfather—Grandfather—" I gulped.

Holding me in thin, strong, old hands, he looked at me long and shrewdly with his faded, shrunken eyes.

"So it's happened, has it?"

"Yes. Yes. It has. But what *is* it, Grandfather? *What* has happened?"

"Easy. Easy!" He soothed me with his voice, as if I had been a panicky foal. "It was bound to come. It always does. Your father— your brothers—now you. All our family. It always happens, sooner or later."

"But what? But what?"

A terrific fusillade of clangs came from the forge. Uncle Josef had the shoe back on the anvil and was reshaping it with powerful blows of his hammer. A fan of sparks rained out, making the carthorse stamp and whinny.

"Come along," said my grandfather. "We'll walk to the church." He put his hand on my shoulder to hoist himself into a walking position and then kept it there, for balance. He was very stooped and walked with a limp; still, for his years, he was as strong as an old root.

We went slowly along the village street. Marigolds blazed; nasturtiums climbed up the sides of the ancient timbered houses. Apples on the trees were almost ripe. The sky, though as cloudless and blue as a gentian, was covered with a light haze; in the mornings and evenings now, mist lay thick in the valley. It was September.

"Winter is coming," said my grandfather.

"Yes, Grandfather."

"Winter is a kind of night," he said. "For months we are prisoners here in the village. As, at night, we are shut in our homes. The next village is a world's end away."

It was true. Our village lies in a deep valley. Often in the winter the roads are blocked with snow for weeks, sometimes for months. Up till now I had never minded this. It was a lot of fun, being closed away from the world. We had huge stacks of firewood—cellars full of wine and flour. The cows and sheep were stabled safely. We had dried fruit, stored apples, fiddles, music, jokes, and a few books. We had each other. What more did we need? Up till now I had loved the winter. But at this moment I shivered as I pictured miles of gale-scoured hills, the snow sent by wind into long, curving drifts, with never a human footprint. Darkness over the mountains for 13 hours, from sunset to sunrise.

"Night is a kind of death," said my grandfather. And then, "You know that I have bad dreams."

Indeed I *did*. His yells when he woke from one of those legendary dreams were terrible to hear; they almost made the blood run backward in your veins. Yet he would never tell us what the dreams had been about; he would sit (once he was awake) white, panting, shaking, gasping, by his bed; sometimes he might have hurled himself right out of his cot, an arm's length away from it, and, the next day, would be covered in black bruises and his eyes sunken in deep gray hollows.

But what the dream was about, he would never reveal. Except perhaps to his old dog, Flag, who had trotted behind us, never more than a yard away, along the village street. During the hours of daylight, Flag never left my grandfather; and at night, when all of the dogs were left downstairs to guard the house and the livestock in the back stable, Flag invariably seemed to know beforehand if my grandfather was going to have one of his bad dreams; in his own sleep he would whine and snuffle; or, often, he would be awake and trembling at the stair foot all night long. And, the next day, Grandfather, as bruised, breathless, staring, and shaky as he was, would be especially kind to Flag and feed him crusts of brown bread dipped in schnapps and honey.

"You know that I have bad dreams," repeated my grandfather.

"Yes, Opar; I know that. We all know it. And we are very sorry for you."

It seemed unfair that such a good, kind man should have such dreadful dreams. All of his harmless life had been lived in the village. All of his deeds were known. Never had he raised his hand unjustly or spoken in malice against another man. Why should *he* have to suffer such an affliction?

We came to the small graveyard where, under wooden crosses and between browsing goats, lay his father, my great-grandfather, and *his* father, and all of my great-uncles and great-great-uncles and so on, back into the past for hundreds of years.

My grandfather looked gravely and gently at the crosses, as if they were old companions from a whole series of hard-fought battles.

"What do we know about being dead?" he said. "Nothing, really."

Old Flag lay down, panting, and Grandfather sat on the low wall. Then he gave me a severe look.

"You don't have any friends," he said.

"Well—how can I, Grandfather? There just isn't anybody my age. Everybody else in the village is either too old for me or too young."

He sighed. "Yes; that's true enough. But tell me now—and tell the truth—when you are by yourself, as you were this afternoon, do you have a made-up friend in your own mind, a dream friend, a wish friend, who comes and talks to you?"

I blushed.

"Yes—well—just sometimes—not very often—"

"One friend—or several?"

"One."

My imaginary friend, Milo, who kept me company sometimes, and laughed at my jokes, and praised me if I had done well in my lessons with Father Tomas.

"Send that being away!" said my grandfather strongly. "Send him away and never never let him come again. Such friends are— can be—very, very dangerous!"

"But, Grandfather, why?"

"Have you ever thought about your brothers?" he said. "Have you ever wondered why Anatol went to be a monk, why Peter joined the army?"

My brothers were many years older than myself. To be

honest, I had never wondered about them at all.

"To be like my father—like Uncle Christian?" I suggested.

Grandfather carefully filled his pipe with strong, sweet-smelling tobacco.

"To be like them—yes," he said between puffs as he lit it. "But also for the same reason. No doubt your brother Peter will be killed, as your father was. No doubt Anatol will be lost to us, as your Uncle Christian was. But this is the reason why they went: a soldier is never alone, for he is always surrounded by other soldiers. Likewise, a monk is never alone, for he is with other monks."

"And in the company of God, too?" I suggested.

"Humph! That depends on the man, I'd say." Grandfather stared, frowning, at the small ancient church, as if he did not quite know where to fit it into the picture that was forming in his mind. Then he went on. "The men of our family do not dare be alone."

"I don't understand—"

"Something happened, once, to our ancestor—"

"Which ancestor?"

"Nobody knows. It was many generations ago. He was a clever man, whoever he was, much more book-learned than the people of his time. He found out something that he should not have."

"What sort of thing? What did he find out?"

"We don't know. But it made him, the first in the family, terrified to be alone."

Impulsively, I started to speak and then closed my mouth. I myself had just encountered that fear, for the first time; I did not wish even to think of it.

"Has it ever occurred to you to wonder," said my grandfather, "what it would be like if you were alone in the world, in an empty room, in an empty house, in a deserted town; if you had reason to be certain that nowhere, not anywhere in the whole world, there was another living being?"

I had never thought of such a possibility. I did now and shivered at the chill of it.

"There you are," said my grandfather, "waiting in the empty house, in the empty street, in the empty world. And yet, now, *Something* comes and taps on the door."

I clutched his hand.

"How *can* it? What *is* that Something?"

"That Something," said my grandfather, "is what stands waiting, now, down in the deepest cellar of your mind."

I let out a sharp cry.

"No! It has no right! I won't have it! I can't bear it!"

"You have to bear it," said Grandfather. "There is no reason to suppose that you, out of the whole family, will be spared."

"Then I'll—I'll—I'll join the army. Like Father, like Peter."

But I knew that I would not.

"No," he said. "You have to stay and work the smithy. With your mother's brothers."

"But what *is* the Something? Why is it so dreadful? Is it," I said hopefully, "is it just because we don't know what it is that it seems dreadful?"

"No," said Grandfather, quenching that hope. "It is dreadful. My dreams tell me that. It is dreadful, and it waits for all of us."

*It has waited a long time for you, Grandfather*, I thought. *Ninety years.*

And he spoke, echoing my thought.

"It has waited ninety years for me."

"But perhaps it won't ever get you, after all, Grandfather."

Flag whimpered dolefully at our feet, and Grandfather looked down and rubbed his ears.

"We must go home," he said. "It will be suppertime, and your mother will be wondering where you have gotten to."

"But what can I do about the—the thing, Grandfather? What can I do?"

"You can be brave," he said.

We walked back between the old houses with their gay flowers. Twilight was thickening in the air. My uncles had long done shoeing the carthorse, and the forge fire had been banked for the night; the tools were put away. I picked up my basket of dried, shriveled lily roots and trudged beside my grandfather in silence.

"Grandfather?" I said after a while.

"Well?"

"Why no imaginary friends?"

"Because," he said, "because—knowing your deep need—they could gain great power over you. And might in the end become the Terror themselves. You must learn to stand quite alone."

"I can't bear it," I said again, and he said again, "You have to bear it."

My grandfather died that night, quickly and quietly, in his sleep. Uncle Josef discovered him in the morning, cold and stiff already—lying straight in his bed for once, with his hands composedly crossed on his breast.

For three days I felt unbelievably wretched, as if my own two hands had been cut off at the wrists. Grandfather had told me so many things, had looked after me so long, had treated me more like a son than a grandson; how could I ever get along in life without him?

And then too there was the aching sense of guilt and worry; had I, with my questions and confessions, with my clamor and my need, somehow laid too heavy a load on him and so hastened his end?

But Father Tomas the priest told me that Grandfather was a man of sterling qualities, a brave, thoughtful, honest, generous man who died in the fullness of years; we should not grieve too much for him, but should be proud of his life and happy that he had gone to a better place.

This comforted me, for a while.

We have this custom when somebody dies that for three days they lie in the church, on a stone bier, with the empty coffin waiting below. Then the priest blesses the coffin, and the burial takes place.

So it was with Grandfather. For three days he lay in the

church. Every morning the people who had loved him came to cover his body with new flowers, asters and late roses and marigolds and trails of scarlet bryony berries and bunches of golden cherry leaves. He looked like a warrior garlanded with wreaths of victory.

And during that time I thought, *All is well with Grandfather.*

But on the third night old Flag, who had lain for days like a stone dog, with his head on his paws, who would not eat nor drink nor let out any sound—on the third evening Flag began to howl. At the stair foot he howled and howled, dementedly, until Uncle Josef said at last, "For God's sake, put the beast outside—this is not to be borne!"

So he was turned loose in the street and ran back and forth across the village all night, howling as if a pack of fiends was at his heels.

In the morning I found him crouched against the church door, shivering and whining. I tied him to a tree and raced to fetch Father Tomas, who unlocked the church door and went inside.

Waiting on the step, I heard him let out a great cry, and so I followed him inside the church, my heart thudding.

There lay Grandfather on the stone floor, a whole man's length away from the bier. The dead flowers were scattered around him, some crushed beneath him.

He must have hurled himself off the stone table and clean over his coffin, which lay on the floor below.

He must have had another dream.

"But he was dead. He was *dead*. I should know; I have seen so many dead people. He has been dead for three days," Father Tomas kept repeating, and he crossed himself, over and over.

He sprinkled Grandfather's body with holy water, and the uncles came and helped him put it inside the coffin and nail down the lid.

The funeral was a hasty, furtive affair. Nobody looked at anybody else. Nobody spoke, besides the usual prayers and psalms. And when it was over, the people dispersed to their own homes without the usual feast, without even loitering for conversation.

Back at home, I huddled in a corner, with my arms around old Flag, and fed him bread dipped in honey and schnapps.

"What did he dream, old Flag? Do you know? Did he dream about Something?"

But old Flag only whined in reply.

I have a puppy now, one of his children's children, and he follows me wherever I go. And I am glad for his company, against the day, not too far now, I think, when it will be *my* turn to dream about Something.

# THE HAND

## GUY DE MAUPASSANT

THEY HAD GATHERED in a circle around Monsieur Bermutier, the magistrate, who was expressing his opinion of the mysterious Saint-Cloud affair. For a whole month this inexplicable crime had been the talk of all of Paris. Nobody could make head or tail of it.

Standing with his back to the fireplace, Monsieur Bermutier was talking away, marshaling evidence, discussing the various theories, but not reaching any conclusion.

Several women had gotten up and drawn closer. They stood around him, their eyes fixed on the magistrate's clean-shaven lips, which were uttering such solemn words. They shuddered and trembled, thrilled by that combination of fear and curiosity, that eager and insatiable love of being frightened that haunts the minds of women and torments them like a hunger.

There was a moment of silence. Then one of them, paler than the others, said, "It's terrifying! It seems like something supernatural. We shall never get to the bottom of it."

The magistrate turned toward her.

"Yes, madame. We probably never shall. But as for this word

'supernatural' that you've just used, it doesn't apply in this case. We are dealing with a crime that was so cleverly thought out— and so cleverly carried out—so thoroughly wrapped up in mystery—that we cannot disentangle it from the baffling circumstances that surround it. But I once had to deal with a case that really *did* seem to have something supernatural about it. We had to abandon it, as a matter of fact, because there was simply no way of clearing it up."

Several of the womenfolk suddenly exclaimed, all at the same time, "Oh, *do* tell us about it!"

Monsieur Bermutier smiled the serious smile that befits an investigating magistrate and went on:

"Now, you mustn't imagine for a moment that I personally give a supernatural explanation to anything in this story. I believe only in natural causes. It would be much better if we simply used the word 'inexplicable' instead of the word 'supernatural' to describe what we do not understand. In any case, in the affair I am going to tell you about it was the circumstances that led up to it that I found so fascinating. At any rate, here are the facts ...

"At that time I was the investigating magistrate in Ajaccio, a little white town situated in a wonderful bay in Corsica, surrounded on all sides by high mountains.

"My particular job there was the investigation of vendettas. Some of them are sublime, ferocious, heroic, incredibly dramatic. In them you come across the finest stories of revenge imaginable, hatreds that have lasted for centuries—dying down for a while, but never extinguished—detestable trickery, murders amounting to massacre and almost becoming something they take pride in. For two years I had heard talk of nothing else but the price of blood and this terrible Corsican tradition that compels a man who has been wronged to take his revenge on the man who has wronged him and on his descendants and relations. I have seen old men, children, cousins—all slaughtered. I used to have my mind filled with incidents of this kind.

"Now, one day I heard that an Englishman had just rented a little villa at the far end of the bay—and had taken a lease for several years. He had brought with him a French manservant whom he had taken into his service while passing through Marseilles.

"Soon everybody was taking an interest in this strange character who lived alone and never went out, except to go hunting and fishing. He never spoke to anybody, never came into town, and every morning he would spend an hour or two in shooting practice, with pistol and rifle.

"Legends began to grow around him. It was claimed that he was a person of some importance who had fled his homeland for political reasons. Then people asserted that he was in hiding because he had committed some dreadful crime. They even supplied particularly horrible details.

"In my official capacity I tried to obtain some information about this man, but I found it impossible to learn anything—except that he called himself Sir John Rowell.

"So I had to remain content with keeping a close watch on him—though, in fact, I had never received reports of anything suspicious concerning him.

"However, as the rumors grew worse and became more widespread, I made up my mind to see this stranger for myself and started to make regular shooting expeditions in the neighborhood of his property.

"It was a long time before I had my opportunity, but at last it presented itself in the form of a partridge that I shot at and killed, right under the Englishman's nose, as it were. My dog brought the bird to me, but I took it right away to Sir John Rowell and asked him to accept it, at the same time apologizing for having disturbed him with my shooting.

"He was a big man with red hair and a red beard, tall and broad-shouldered, a sort of calm, well-mannered giant. He had none of the so-called British stiffness, and he thanked me warmly for being so civil, speaking with a strong English accent. During the following month we chatted together five or six times.

"Then one evening, as I was passing his gate, I saw him smoking his pipe, sitting astride a chair in the garden. I greeted him, and he invited me into the garden to drink a glass of beer. I didn't need asking twice!

"He greeted me with all of the meticulous courtesy typical of the English, was full of praise for France and Corsica, and said, in very bad French, how fond he was of 'cette pays' [this country] and 'cette rivage' [this stretch of coast].

"Then I began to inquire about his past life and his plans for the future, asking my questions very tactfully and making a show of genuine interest in his affairs. He replied without any sign of embarrassment and told me that he had traveled a good deal in Africa, India, and America. He added, with a laugh, 'I've had plenty of adventures. I have indeed!'

"When I brought the conversation back to the subject of hunting, he began to tell me all sorts of interesting things about the hunting of hippos, tigers, elephants—and even gorillas.

"'Those are all fearful brutes,' I said.

"'Oh, no!' he said with a smile. 'The worst brute of all is man!' And he gave the hearty laugh of a big, genial Englishman, and then he added, 'I've often hunted man, too.'

"Then he began to talk about guns, and he invited me to come inside the house and see the various types of guns he had.

"His drawing room was draped in black—black silk, embroidered with big golden flowers that were scattered over the somber material, gleaming like flames.

"'The silk is from Japan,' he said.

"But in the middle of the largest panel a strange object attracted my attention: it was black and stood out clearly against a square of red velvet. I went up to it. It was a hand, a human hand—not the hand of a skeleton, all white and clean, but a black, withered hand, with yellow nails, exposed muscles, and traces of congealed blood, looking like dirt. The bones had been chopped off at around the middle of the forearm, as though they had been severed by an ax.

"An enormous iron chain was riveted and welded into the wrist of this filthy limb and at the other end was attached to the wall by a ring strong enough to hold an elephant.

"I asked him, 'What's that?'

"The Englishman calmly replied, 'That's my worst enemy. It came from America. It was chopped off with a saber, skinned with a sharp bit of stone, and then dried in the sun for a week. And a damn good job it was too!'

"I touched this human relic. It must have belonged to a man of gigantic size. The fingers, which were abnormally long, were held in place by enormous tendons that had fragments of skin still clinging to them. The hand—flayed like this—was a frightening thing to see. You could not help thinking that it was the result of some barbaric act of vengeance.

"I remarked, 'This man must have been very strong.'

"The Englishman replied in a gentle voice, 'Oh, yes. But I was stronger than he was. I fixed that chain on his hand to prevent it from escaping.'

"I thought he must be joking, so I said, 'That chain won't be much use now. The hand won't run away!'

"Sir John Rowell then said in a very serious voice, 'It's *always* trying to get away. That chain is necessary.'

"I took a quick glance at his face, saying to myself, 'Is the fellow a madman—or a practical joker?'

"But his face remained inscrutable, with its placid, benevolent expression. So I changed the subject and began to admire his guns.

"I noticed, however, that three loaded revolvers had been placed on various items of furniture, as if this man was living in constant fear of being attacked.

"I made several more visits to his home, and then I stopped

going there. We had become accustomed to his presence, and people now paid little attention to him.

"A whole year went by. Then, one morning, toward the end of November, my servant woke me with the news that Sir John Rowell had been murdered during the night.

"Half an hour later I was entering the Englishman's house, along with the chief magistrate and the captain of the local police. Sir John's manservant, bewildered and in despair, was standing at the door in tears. At first I suspected this man—but he turned out to be innocent. We never did discover who the murderer was.

"When I entered Sir John's drawing room, the first thing I saw was the corpse lying on its back in the middle of the room.

"His waistcoat had been torn; a sleeve of his jacket had been ripped away; everything pointed to the fact that a terrible struggle had taken place.

"The Englishman had been choked to death! His face was black and swollen—a terrifying sight—and the expression on it suggested that he had experienced the most appalling horror. There was something between his tightly clenched teeth, and in his neck, which was covered with blood, there were five puncture marks. They looked as though they had been made by fingers of iron.

"A doctor arrived. He spent a long time examining the imprints of the fingers in the flesh and then came out with the strange remark: 'You'd think he'd been strangled by a skeleton!'

"A shudder ran down my spine, and immediately I looked at the place on the wall where I had previously seen the horrible flayed hand. It was no longer there. The broken chain was hanging down.

"Then I bent over the corpse. In his twisted mouth I found one of the fingers of the missing hand. It had been cut off—or rather sawn off—by the dead man's teeth, exactly at the second joint.

"We got on with our investigations. But we could discover nothing. No door or window had been forced; nothing had been broken into. The two guard dogs had not even awakened.

"Very briefly, this is the statement made by the servant. He said that for the past month his master had seemed very upset. He had received a lot of letters that he had burned as soon as they arrived. Often he had picked up a horsewhip, and, in a display of anger that bordered on insanity, he had furiously beaten that withered hand that had been riveted to the wall and that had, somehow or other, been removed at the very hour that the crime was committed. Sir John used to go to bed very late, and he would carefully lock all of the doors and windows. He always kept firearms within easy reach. Often, at night, he had been heard talking in a loud voice, as though he was quarreling with someone . . .

"On that particular night, as it happens, he had not made a sound, and it was only when he came to open the windows the next morning that the servant had found Sir John lying there, murdered. There was nobody this servant could think of as a suspect.

"I told the magistrates and police officers everything I knew about the dead man, and the most detailed inquiries were made over the whole island. Nothing was discovered.

"Now, one night, three months after the murder, I had a dreadful nightmare. I thought that I saw the hand, the horrible hand, running like a scorpion or a spider, all over the curtains and walls of my room. Three times I woke up, three times I fell asleep again, three times I saw that hideous human relic crawling rapidly around my bedroom, using its fingers as a creature uses its legs.

"In the morning this hand was brought to me. They had found it in the cemetery, lying on Sir John's grave. He had been buried on the island because they had not been able to trace his family. The hand had the index finger missing.

"Well, ladies. There's my story. That's all I know."

The women who had been listening were horrified and looked pale and trembling. One of them exclaimed, "But that's not a proper ending! You haven't given us an explanation! We shall not be able to get to sleep tonight unless you tell us your opinion of what really happened."

The magistrate gave his austere smile. "Oh, ladies, I'm afraid that I am going to deprive you of your nightmares! I simply think that the lawful owner of the hand was still alive and that he came to get back his severed hand by using the one that remained. The only thing is, I just haven't been able to find out how he did it. It was obviously a sort of vendetta."

One of the women murmured, "No, that *can't* be the real explanation." And the magistrate, still smiling, finally remarked, "Well, I warned you that my theory wouldn't satisfy you!"

# THE BOY NEXT DOOR

### ELLEN EMERSON WHITE

WINTER, IN NEW England, was much too cold for ice cream. But the show must go on, the store must stay open, and Dorothy was working from four to nine. The closing shift. It was boring to work by herself, but they weren't getting enough business for her boss to justify paying extra staff.

It was *very* boring.

A few parents—divorced fathers, mostly—brought their kids for prebedtime cones; some sorority girls from the university rushed in to get a cake for a birthday that had been forgotten. She talked them into the 12-inch, instead of the nine, because they were supposed to sell up. When someone asked for a cone of chocolate chip or whatever, she was supposed to say, "Yes, sir, would that be a medium?" Because suggesting a large cone would make customers nervous and inclined to say, "No, no, just a small." But "medium" sounded so—so *harmless*. So average.

The same way a dollar 99 sounded so much less expensive than two dollars.

As memory served, W. C. Fields had a theory about that.

Two couples came in, double-dating. The girls were, quite

vocally, watching their weight, so they decided on small diet Cokes. The guys didn't seem too happy about that, and there was a lot of discussion before all four of them finally ordered sundaes. "No nuts on mine," one of the girls added quickly, which would be a not-inconsiderable saving in calories, considering that they were butter-toasted—but a rather paltry saving, in the scheme of the overall sundae.

Dorothy, however, just kept her mouth shut and made the sundaes. Rang them up. Gave back the change. Rinsed the two scoops that she'd used.

Business was slow and dull. Although there were worse things than getting paid minimum wage for doing physics homework.

Around 7:30, her friend Jill came in. Best friend, actually. They had met in kindergarten and become instantly inseparable because they were the only two in the class who could read, and looking at d-o-g and c-a-t flash cards was dull. "Ennui," Jill had said, more than once. "Our friendship is *founded* on ennui."

Not that she had a flair for the dramatic or anything.

In many ways, they were exact opposites—Jill was tall, she was short; Jill was blonde, she had dark hair; Jill liked art, she liked science—but by the time they had gotten around to noticing that they had very little in common, they were already such close friends that it didn't matter.

"So," Jill said, leaning heavily against the counter, "what do I get free?"

Dorothy grinned and pointed in the direction of the drinking fountain.

"Think I'll pass," Jill said and took off her mittens. Lumpy-looking mittens, but, then again, she'd made them herself, and Dorothy had to give points for that. "It's really *cold* out—are people actually coming in here?"

Dorothy shook her head. "No."

Jill hung over the glass counter, looking at the various tubs. "Is that one new?" she asked, pointing.

"Yeah, licorice." Dorothy reached for a little wooden paddle. "Want to try it? It's even worse than pumpkin."

Jill tasted a spoonful and then nodded. "It's almost as bad as cinnamon crunch."

Dorothy nodded, took back the paddle, and threw it away.

Jill unzipped her jacket slightly and then zipped it back up. "I was kind of surprised there were so many people," she said.

The funeral. "Small town," Dorothy said. Almost everyone knew everyone else, so when someone died—or was born—or played Little League—or had a yard sale—a lot of people showed up. So even though Mrs. Creighton had been an absolutely *terrible* teacher—a complete terror, when you got right down to it—the church had been packed. The funeral had been over the weekend—but that didn't mean that everyone wasn't still talking about it.

"Yeah," Jill said and frowned. "I'm just always surprised. I mean, no one likes you while you're alive, but then you *die*, and suddenly, everyone's lining up to give eulogies. It's strange."

Dorothy nodded. Very strange.

"I really don't *like* funerals," Jill said.

Dorothy nodded. No argument there.

"Well." Jill straightened up. "Think you'll get out of here in time for 'Miss America'?"

Dorothy looked around the empty store. "Unless I get a rush."

"Right." Jill grinned and also looked around. "Well, if you do, come by or call me up—I have a feeling it's Miss Rhode Island's year."

Highly unlikely. "I'm going with the Pacific Northwest," Dorothy said. "Miss—Oregon, maybe." Not that she had any idea of what any of the contestants looked like. Or, really, even cared much.

"Not a chance," Jill said. "Unless they have really good talent." She paused. "I can't remember why we wait all year to watch it."

Well—not for the baton twirling. "Because we each, secretly, want to be Miss Congeniality," Dorothy said.

"Oh. Right." Jill put her mittens back on and headed for the door. "Don't work too hard."

Dorothy nodded and, finished with her physics homework, reached for her calculus book.

The store manager, Howard, stopped by at 8:30 to grumble about the lack of money in the register and take most of it back to the safe. Then he came back out to remind her about turning off the heat under the hot fudge and butterscotch, being sure to rotate the ice-cream sandwiches when she restocked, and to remember to turn on the alarm system before she left.

She nodded, already at work refilling the jimmies. Sprinkles. Ants. Everyone who came in had a different name for them.

By the time she'd locked up, promptly at nine o'clock, she only had to tip up the chairs on top of the tables, mop the floor, and spray clean the glass on the display cases.

Howard hated fingerprints. Small children sometimes even left *face* prints.

It was ten after nine when someone knocked on the door. She pointed to the CLOSED sign and then saw that it was Matt Wilson—whom she had known since third grade. They had even gone on a date—once—to the movies. Freddy Krueger. Not exactly her idea of a thrill, although Matt had liked it just fine. She had kissed him, pleasantly, good night, and since then, they had treated each other with mutual, vague disinterest. Had some of the same classes, ended up at the same football parties, said hi if they ran into each other at the mall. Other than that, they rarely spoke.

She didn't particularly want to let him in—but if she didn't, it was the sort of thing that would get around school, and everyone would think she was a—do you really *care* what people think? Jill would say. And she would probably answer that she did more than she didn't.

Besides, it was pretty cold out there.

"Hi," she said, unlocking the door. "I kind of have to close up."

Matt nodded, coming in. Since she remembered him as a skinny ten year old in maroon Toughskins jeans, it was always sort of a shock to realize that he was six feet tall now, had a much deeper voice—and possibly even shaved. Hard to believe it was the same guy who had thrown up on the bus—all *over* the bus—

when they had gone on a field trip to the aquarium in the sixth grade.

"You want anything?" she asked. "Before I finish scooping down?" She went back behind the counter—and back to the chocolate walnut fudge, which was frozen rock-solid and unyielding.

"They make you work alone?" he asked.

"Well—we aren't exactly thriving lately," she said, gesturing toward the empty parking lot. Well, empty except for her parents' station wagon.

Matt nodded, looking around. Shifting his weight from one high-top to the other. Looking around some more.

Call her prescient, but she was getting a bad feeling here. "Uh, Matt?" she said. "I can make you something fast, but then I really have to lock up."

Now he looked at her, and—his eyes seemed a little funny. Too bright or—too *something*. Jumpy. "I want to see what it's like," he said, quietly.

Make that a *very* bad feeling. "Oh, yeah?" she said. "The thing is, my manager's going to show up, and if you're in here, I'm going to get in trouble."

He shook his head.

"Come on." She started to move out from behind the counter again. "I don't want to lose my job."

He shook his head. "I saw him. He already left."

He'd been watching. Great. And her car was the only one out there, so he must have parked somewhere else. Must have been *planning* this. Whatever it was.

She glanced down at the little metal ice-cream spatula that she was holding—it wasn't much, as weapons went—and then glanced in the direction of the wall phone. A good 15 feet. And it had a *dial*, not pushbuttons, so it would take her longer to get an operator.

Well, gosh.

Time to be distracting. After all, she'd known the guy since *third grade*. How dangerous could he really be? "Matt, if you don't take off," she said, "I'm never going to make it home in time for 'Miss America.'"

He just looked at her.

"And—neither are you," she said.

He didn't say anything.

Keep talking. "Well, okay, I see your point," she said, nodding. "You've probably already missed the swimsuits."

He looked at her with very little expression. Slight eagerness, maybe. "Open the register."

She stared at him. "What?"

"*Open* the register," he said.

This was scary—but this was also weird. "What do you mean?" she asked. "There's almost nothing in there. No one buys ice cream in weather like this."

"*Open* the damn register," he said.

"Oh, and give you the whole twenty dollars?" she asked. "If there's even that much."

His fist came out, unexpectedly, and knocked the glass

donation jar off the counter. It landed with a shattering crash, change rolling all over the floor. Which was scary, but it made her a little mad, too.

"That's for crippled children," she said. "You really going to take money from *crippled children*?"

He looked at her with the same strange—blank—expression.

"On top of which," she said, "I *just* swept."

He came over the counter with an easy athletic motion, landing right in front of her. And, under the circumstances, it occurred to her that six feet was pretty big. A good ten inches—and at least 80 pounds—bigger than she was.

The small metal spatula probably wasn't going to tip the odds.

Not that it wouldn't be worth a try. But—she would keep it as a trump card.

"Matt, this is really weird," she said. "Are Nicky and Fred and all those guys outside, and you're all just pulling my leg here? Because I *really* want to close up."

He reached inside his jacket pocket—expensive Gore-Tex—and brought out a gun. A handgun. Which he pointed at her. "I want to know what it's like," he said.

Well, this was just going from bad to worse, wasn't it? "Why don't you help yourself to the twenty," she said, indicating the register. "Take the money for muscular dystrophy, too. In fact," she said and pulled a five-dollar bill out of her jeans, "take this. Get yourself a couple of Big Macs."

He didn't even seem to hear that, holding the gun and smiling slightly. "I've *always* wanted to know what it's like," he said. This had moved beyond weird, past ominous, and straight to dire. The thing to do was stay calm. "I don't know, Matt," Dorothy said, putting back the five-dollar bill. "This is turning into a bad 'Afterschool Special,' know what I mean?"

Since he was just standing there, smiling—he probably didn't know what she meant.

Okay. Time to go into a holding pattern. Since she *really* wasn't enjoying looking at a gun that might—might not?—be loaded. "Well," she said, "I think I'll—"

He stuck the gun into the back of her uniform shirt. "I think you'll shut up."

Okay. She shut up.

"I'll take the money," he said and twisted the spatula out of her hand. It fell into the ice-cream case, out of reach. "After. To make it look like a robbery."

"Okay," she said, checking the quiet street outside. Since everything was closed, there wasn't much reason for anyone to drive by. Even one of the few town police cars. "But you'd better hurry, because my father's going to be coming to pick me up."

He jabbed the gun into her back and then pointed with it at her car, out in the snowy parking lot.

"I know," she said. "Dead battery."

He jabbed her, harder, with the gun. "Shut up."

Well—it had been worth a try. She shrugged and shut up. There was going to be a point at which she was going to have to take this situation a little more seriously—start *panicking*—but she wasn't there yet. This was, after all, a guy who had always tried, and failed, to cheat off her in eighth-grade earth science.

"I'm going to kill you," he said.

There it was—her cue to take this seriously.

"See"—his smile widened a little—"I've always wondered what it would be like—you know, to kill someone—so, I'm going to do it. Find out. And the police'll just think it's a robbery, see?"

Uh-huh. She edged a step away from him.

"I really want to. Always have," he said. "I've been thinking about it for a long time and—you know, what it would *feel* like— and I think—" He grinned, a little. "I've been planning this, you know?"

Well—she certainly knew now. "Boy," she said, keeping her voice calm, "and people say it isn't dangerous for MTV to show all those violent images."

He didn't seem to think that was funny. Somehow, she wasn't surprised.

"Look, I don't know if you're kidding, Matt," she said, "but, either way, I think you should consider *intensive* psychotherapy."

He didn't seem to think that was funny either.

"Okay if I sit down for a minute, Matt?" she asked. "Considering how long we've known each other?"

"Sure." He laughed again. "We got at least thirty minutes, an hour, I figure, before anyone thinks it's funny that the lights are still on in here."

It would also probably be that long before her parents got

THE BOY NEXT DOOR

worried enough to call or show up. They didn't like the idea that she closed up alone on weeknights. They were always afraid that something—bad—might happen.

In the future, she was going to have to take those sorts of concerns more seriously.

"On the floor," he said. "So no one will see us if they go by. Right there." He indicated for her to sit down against the counter, and then he sat down too, looking pleased with himself, his back resting against the soft-serve machine.

Her head hurt, in a numb sort of way. "Want a dish of cinnamon crunch?" she asked. "It's really good."

He scowled at her. "You'd better start being scared. It's not as fun if you're not scared."

Exactly. She resisted the urge to rub her temples. "So, if you're a robber, how'd you get in? Would I really have opened the door?"

He gestured with the gun. "I'll break the glass on my way out."

Oh. "Wouldn't I have heard you?" she asked.

"I'll turn up the radio," he said.

Oh.

"See," he said, his eyes brightening even more, "it looks *fun*. When they do it. When you see movies of it and all. So I want to see what it's like. To do it."

What had he been doing, sitting at home watching reenactments on *America's Most Wanted*? Taping shows like that, so he could watch them over and over? He seemed so normal, the neighbors would say. So polite. The boy next door. "Shouldn't you work your way up?" she asked. "Start off by—I don't know—throwing rocks at seagulls?"

He smiled. "I killed a dog."

Oh. She rubbed her hand across her forehead. Thought thoughts about aspirin.

"But, you know, I didn't *feel* anything," he said. "I didn't feel good, or bad, or—maybe 'cause I used a car. Maybe if I'd really *done* it, myself, I—so I'm really going to *do* this. And—then I'll know."

The thing she had to keep in mind here was that Matt Wilson wasn't exactly the brightest guy she had ever known. So—keep him talking. "Did we really have that bad a time on our date?" she asked.

He didn't say anything, just stood there, looking at her, holding the gun with great confidence. Familiarity. Pleasure.

Well, "Quick on the uptake" wasn't going to go on his tombstone. "I don't want to be trite," she said, "but, why me?" Such a nice boy, the elderly neighbor would tell Maury Povich. Always shoveled my walk.

"Because—you're not special," he said.

Oh. Not exactly the answer that she had expected. Her breath got stuck somewhere inside her throat, and it was an effort to swallow.

"You know what I mean?" he said, leaning forward. "You're just—you're just *there*. Like, I know you, and I see you around, but—I don't give you any thought. Like, if you weren't there, I don't think I'd really notice." He frowned. "I don't think anyone really will. After the first couple weeks, or—maybe not even *that* long. You know?"

"The feeling's mutual," she said stiffly. Nice to have her entire existence reduced to a footnote. A memorial page in the yearbook. *If* that.

"Like," he said, not even seeming to hear her, too far into his own crazed little reverie, "they'll be sad at school, at *first*, and they'll have, you know, counselors come, so everyone can *talk* about how sad they are, and then—" He snapped his fingers. "Next thing you know, spring training'll be starting."

The fact that he just might be right was almost more terrifying than the rest of this. People's lives *were* getting pretty disposable these days. Even if you died in a really *interesting* way, you *still* might not make the evening news.

"So, I do you," he said, "and—big deal. They shouldn't've had you working here alone at night. 'Cause—you got robbed by some hopped-up junkie with a"—he made his hand shake on the gun—"quick trigger finger."

He *had* been thinking about this. What a waste of limited brainpower. Because—it *would* look like a robbery gone bad. Like her mother always said, plenty of bad things happened in small towns, not just big cities, but the difference was, in the small town, you *knew* the people.

Her head hurt. She wanted to go home. The floor was filthy. "What about fingerprints?" she asked.

He grinned. "Haven't touched anything. And if I do have

to—" With his free hand, he took a pair of winter gloves out of his pocket to show her.

"Well." She leaned back against the cold white counter. There was a small chocolate smudge, maybe knee-high. "That's good. You've thought of—almost everything."

"I've thought of *everything*," he said and glanced at his watch. "I want you to lie down now. Hands behind your head."

Oh, great. Execution-style. He must have been renting gangster movies. It was important to keep in mind that she really was smarter than he was. Maybe not *special*, but definitely smarter. "What you haven't thought about," she said, "is what it's *really* like to kill someone. It *is* easy, but it's pointless. Even if it's personal."

He scowled at her. "Shut up. I'm getting tired of you."

"Yeah, but"—she lowered her voice, carefully, as though there was someone else around to hear—"I know what I'm talking about."

He scowled at her, but uneasily.

Okay, good. Keep it up. "Even if the person probably *should* die," she said. "Even if you have a *serious* grudge against them, it doesn't seem to matter. Because, it doesn't change anything. You do it, and you don't feel better; you just feel—nothing. Like with the dog. You feel—it's a waste. You risk so much, and you don't get anything back."

"What do *you* know about it?" he asked—but at least he was listening.

Okay, she'd gotten his attention. Time to bring out the big

guns. "I know more than you think," she said. "But—we have to have a deal. If I tell you, you have to leave here, and no one'll ever know about this. Because we'll each have something to hold over each other, so—we can just keep it to ourselves."

He frowned at her suspiciously. "You just don't want me to kill you."

God, he was dense. "Well, *obviously*," she said. "Would I really be stupid enough to tell you about this otherwise?"

He frowned. Pointed the gun. "Tell me what?"

Dorothy took a deep breath and then let it out. "I killed Mrs. Creighton."

He sat up straighter and then shook his head. "Oh, yeah, *right*. Nice try. You're just, like, *stalling*."

No, she was trolling out her line, trying to get him hooked. "You want to hear what it was like?" she asked. "Stuff *nobody* else knows?"

He didn't say yes, but she could tell that he was starting to get a little curious. Intrigued.

"Think about it, Matt," she said. "We were all in her class together." Fifth grade. "Think about what a terrible teacher she was. She was really *mean* to me—remember?"

He frowned. "No. Like, she was mean to everyone."

"Yeah, well, I didn't like it." She paused. For great effect. "And I waited a *long* time to get back at her."

It was quiet for a few seconds, the hum of the freezers sounding loud.

"She was in an accident," Matt said. "Just a dumb accident on

131

the ice."

Dorothy nodded. "That's right. I *wanted* it to look like an accident. The same way you want *this* to look like an accident." Hooked? Or still just nibbling on the bait?

He glanced at his watch and then looked back at her, grinning. "Okay," he said. "Let's see how far you can take this, huh?"

Hooked. "First, promise not to tell anyone," she said.

He laughed. "Like I'm really going to tell anyone what you *said* while I was *killing* you?"

Okay, so she wasn't making as many inroads as she'd thought. "I'm not kidding, Matt," she said. "*I'm* making a deal here. And—admit it. You want to hear about it."

"I'm the one holding the gun," he said. "I'm the only one who can make deals."

"Fine." She folded her arms across her chest. "Go ahead and shoot. Before you run out of time."

He shook his head, looking very amused. Stupidly amused. "No. I want to hear about your big-wow murder plot first."

Well, it was the only hand she had, so she might as well play it out. Go for broke. "You know how the road curves there?" she said. Everyone in town knew about that curve. "Above the ocean? And that's the way she would *have* to drive. To get home. And, well, I know what her car looks like, right? Same way you know that's my parents' car out there in the parking lot."

He frowned, but he *was* still listening.

No matter what a story was about, the important thing was to *tell* it well. With *conviction*. "So, I waited," she said. "In the bushes, there, just around the curve. More than one afternoon, if you want to know the truth. Because—she had to go by—and I figured the best time was right after dusk."

He shook his head, scornfully—but didn't, she noticed, interrupt.

"So no one would see me and so she wouldn't have time to react." She was getting a little stiff and would have stretched, but didn't want to do anything to distract him. "It's a funny thing about that curve," she said. "It really is dangerous, but everyone always drives pretty fast around it. I guess because they know it's there and don't think about it much. I mean, *I* go fast around that curve, don't you?"

He nodded and then frowned and pointed the gun.

Play it out. "So, I waited," she said. "I had a pretty good view, because I wanted to be able to see her coming in plenty of time. And I was trying to think, how could I be sure that she would turn out of the way fast? Be *sure* that she'd go right over onto the rocks there?"

He wasn't looking at her now so much as *watching* her.

"Because—I was only going to get one chance," she said.

He watched her.

"A baby carriage," she said. And paused. "I don't care who you are, no matter where you are—even if it doesn't make sense —if you see a *baby carriage* come out in front of your car, you're going to try not to hit it. Right? Makes sense, doesn't it?"

Matt nodded a little.

"Right," she said. Press on. "So, I waited. And I waited. And Thursday afternoon, right after dark, who should come speeding along?" She paused and then nodded significantly. "Yeah. So, I timed it. Wanted to be sure that she'd *see* it, but only after it was too late. I *timed* it, and then I pushed the carriage out there, and—" She let herself grin with exquisite slowness. "And she swerved, and she went *right off the road*, just like I thought she would."

Matt was watching her with his mouth hanging open, although he probably wasn't aware of it.

Good. Keep going. "I didn't bother looking down over what was left of the guardrail," Dorothy said. "In case she *hadn't* been killed and only—maimed—or something and was looking up. I just went out to the middle of the road, got the baby carriage, and carried it back, through the bushes, to my car, so I could get rid of it." She paused. Slightly longer than briefly. "Evidence—right?"

She checked Matt's expression; he was frowning.

"But, here's the problem," she said. "The problem for you. I *really* didn't like her. I had it *in* for her. And, yeah, she ran off the road, and, yeah, it was because of me, and—it didn't seem to matter. It wasn't a kick. It was just like, so what? I mean, you're right—you and I have absolutely no opinion about each other. So, if you *waste* it on me, take the chance, it's just—stupid. If you have to do it, make it someone you *hate*. Try to make it worth your time and trouble. Make it worth the *risk*."

It was quiet again.

"Nice story," he said and then cocked the gun. "Now, put your hands behind your head."

She'd really thought that she'd had him going along there. "I can *prove* it," she said as he started to get up.

He stopped.

"Because"—keep that brain working quickly— "even when you're sure you've thought of everything, you haven't."

He eased back down, but kept the gun cocked. "So, prove it."

"She *hit* the carriage," Dorothy said. "So, if the police or, I don't know, whoever, checked the bumper, they'd find paint or metal chips that *weren't* from the guardrail."

He shrugged. "So?"

Slap down the last card. Full force. "I'll tell you where the carriage *is*," she said. "So, if I went to the police and said that you came in here and threatened me, *you* could easily tell them that I was lying about it, because you knew about Mrs. Creighton."

He narrowed his eyes at her.

"It's *perfect*," she said. "This way, we're both off the hook. We can both go home and—pretend this never happened."

"Yeah, right," he said. "Like I'm going to fall for *that*."

Yes. He was. "I threw it off the bridge," she said. "Up near the Point? Because, even when the tide goes out and it's just marshy, there's so much junk down there that I knew no one would notice."

He frowned, but indecisively. "I know you're lying."

"We can drive up there," she said. "After school tomorrow. I can *show* you." She almost had him here—she could feel it. So she paused again. "And, if you want—" She paused again. "I'll tell you about the others."

There was no question but that his eyes widened. "The *others*?"

Hook, line, *and* sinker. "Seems to me," she said, "that there's been more than one accident in this town in the last couple of years." Remember to pause. "I can tell you all about them."

"I *know* you're lying," he said, but without much assurance.

She shook her head. "No, you don't. Admit it. You know I'm telling the truth."

He looked at her. *Studied* her.

"You know I am," she said quietly.

There was another long silence, and then, finally, he nodded.

Next stop, National Poker Championships. "Yeah," she said. "I'll tell you about all of them, and then—maybe you and I can do another. *Together*."

He looked at her. Started to grin.

"What the heck," she said. "Maybe it would be more fun that way. If you had someone to *share* it with."

The phone rang, suddenly, and they both jumped.

"What's that?" he asked nervously.

She checked her watch. "My parents. Because I'm running late."

The phone rang again.

"Look, get out of here," she said. "You can't do anything now, because they'll *know* it wasn't a robber. Get out of here, and we can talk at school tomorrow."

The phone had rung again and then again.

"*Go*," she said. "Don't be stupid."

A fifth ring.

He nodded, getting up, and she got up too, answering the phone. Indeed, her mother.

"Oh, hi, Mom," she said. "Yeah, I was down in the basement, getting straws and napkins and all." She motioned toward the door, and Matt nodded.

"Tomorrow?" he said.

She nodded; *he* nodded; and he left.

Left.

All right! Nice *talking*, Tex.

She explained to her mother that she was still cleaning up, was almost done, and got permission to stop by Jill's to watch the end of "Miss America." Then, once she'd hung up, she went over and locked the door. Took the keys and put them in her pocket. Dimmed the lights.

She should probably call the police or have told her mother— but tell them *what*? That the right tackle on the football team suffered from psychosis? Had a violent fantasy life? Was just plain *wacko*? That he'd broken the muscular dystrophy jar? That he had—all she wanted to do right now was get out of here. Then she could worry about how to handle the situation.

She swept up the glass and pennies. Left a note for Howard that the jar had fallen and put the change in an empty box that had once held cans of whipped cream. She put up the chairs, mopped the floor, turned the lights off, and the alarm *on*.

It was 10:15. Seemed later.

She went out to the parking lot and sat in the car. Sat, taking deep breaths, seeing her hands still shaking with reaction, trembling.

*That* had been scary. Really, really *scary*. Unbelievable, in fact. And—she wasn't quite sure what to do. If she should just go home, or—she started the car and pulled out of the parking lot, driving slowly and cautiously on the ice. Headed toward Jill's house.

Jill's little brother, Timmy, let her in.

"You're late," he said cheerfully. "You missed the question-and-answer section."

Dorothy nodded. "Yeah, I know. She in the den?"

"Yep," he said and offered her his bag of Doritos.

"No, thanks," she said and headed for the den.

Jill was sitting in there, alone, wearing her reading glasses, her French book open—and completely ignored—on her lap. "Hi," she said.

Dorothy nodded and sat down in the easy chair.

"Miss Nebraska had a really nice gown," Jill said.

Dorothy nodded, trying to figure out exactly how to explain what had happened tonight. Exactly what to say.

"But her hair was stupid." Jill glanced over for a second. "You all right?"

"Yeah, I—" No. "Um, tonight, uh—while I was closing up, um—" She should just start. Tell her the whole twisted story. "Look, uh—" She let out her breath. "We have to do it again."

Now, Jill looked away from the television. "*What?*"

"Yeah," Dorothy said.

Jill glanced at the television and then took off her glasses. "We can't. She was going to be the last one."

"Yeah, I know, but—" Dorothy sighed. "This will be the last one, okay?"

Jill sighed too. "You sure?"

Dorothy nodded.

"Okay," Jill said and closed her French book. "When?"

Preferably, an hour ago. "After school tomorrow?" Dorothy said.

Jill thought about that and then nodded. "Okay. Who is it, anyway?"

"Matt Wilson," Dorothy said.

Jill grinned. "Whoa. *That* must be a long story."

Very long. Dorothy nodded.

"Well—tell me at the commercial," Jill said and then looked at her. "This is going to be the last one, right?"

Dorothy nodded.

"Good," Jill said and put her glasses back on.

Then they both looked at the television.

# THE MURDER HOLE

## SCOTTISH FOLKTALE

AROUND THREE HUNDRED years ago, on the estate of Lord Cassilis between Ayrshire and Galloway, lay a great moor, unrelieved by any trees or vegetation.

It was rumored that unwary travelers had been intercepted and murdered there and that no investigation ever revealed what had happened to them. People living in a nearby hamlet believed that in the dead of night they sometimes heard a sudden cry of anguish; and a shepherd who had lost his way once declared that he had seen three mysterious figures struggling together, until one of them, with a frightful scream, sank suddenly into the earth. So terrifying was this place that at last no one remained there, except one old woman and her two sons, who were too poor to flee as their neighbors had done. Travelers occasionally begged a night's lodging at their cottage, rather than continue their journey across the moor in the darkness, and even by day no one traveled that way except in companies of at least two or three people.

One stormy November night, a peddler boy was overtaken by darkness on the moor. Terrified by the solitude, he repeated to himself the promises of the Scripture and so struggled toward the old cottage, which he had visited the year before in a large company of travelers and where he felt assured of a welcome. Its light guided him from afar, and he knocked on the door, but at first received no answer. He then peered through a window and saw that the occupants were all at their accustomed occupations: the old woman was scrubbing the floor and scattering it with sand; her two sons seemed to be thrusting something large and heavy into a great chest, which they then hastily locked. There was an air of haste about all of this that puzzled the waiting boy outside.

He tapped lightly on the window, and they all started up with consternation on their faces, and one of the men suddenly darted out at the door, seized the boy roughly by the shoulder, and dragged him inside. He said, trying to laugh, "I am only the poor peddler who visited you last year." *"Are you alone?"* cried the old woman in a harsh, deep voice. "Alone here—and alone in the whole world," replied the boy sadly. "Then you are welcome," said one of the men with a sneer. Their words filled the boy with alarm, and the confusion and desolation of the formerly neat and orderly cottage seemed to show signs of recent violence.

The curtains had been torn down from the bed to which he was shown, and though he begged for a light to burn until he fell asleep, his terror kept him long awake.

In the middle of the night he was awakened by a single cry of distress. He sat up and listened, but it was not repeated, and he would have lain down to sleep again, but suddenly his eye fell on a stream of blood slowly trickling under the door of his room. In terror he sprang to the door, and through a chink he saw that the victim outside was only a goat. But just then he overheard the voices of the two men, and their words transfixed him with horror. "I wish all of the throats we cut were as easy," said one. "Did you ever hear such a noise as the old gentleman made last night?" "Ah, the murder hole's the thing for me," said the other. "One plunge, and the fellow's dead and buried in a moment." "How do you mean to dispatch the lad in there?" asked the old woman in a harsh whisper, and one of the men silently drew his bloody knife across his throat for an answer.

The terrified boy crept to his window and managed to let himself down without a sound. But as he stood wondering which way to turn, a dreadful cry rang out: "The boy has escaped—let loose the bloodhound." He ran for his life, blindly, but all too soon he heard the dreadful baying of the hound and the voices of the men in pursuit. Suddenly he stumbled and fell on a heap of rough stones that cut him on every limb so that his blood poured over the stones. He staggered to his feet and ran on; the hound was so close that he could almost feel its breath on his back. But suddenly it smelled the blood on the stones, and, thinking the chase at an end, it lay down and refused to go farther after the same scent. The boy fled on and on till morning, and when at last he reached a village, his pitiable state and his fearful story roused such wrath that three gibbets were at once set upon the moor, and before night the three villains had been captured and had confessed their guilt. The bones of their victims were later discovered and with great difficulty brought up from the dreadful hole with its narrow aperture into which they had been thrust.

# THE FAMOUS FIVE GO PILLAGING

### TERRY JONES and MICHAEL PALIN

*An exciting tale of children caught up in the Danish invasions*

### *Chapter One: The Collapse of Roman Imperialism*

BILL AND ENID were coming back through Tadger's field when suddenly they saw the collapse of Roman imperialism.

"Gosh," said Bill.

"So, a combination of factors, both economic and social, has brought down the mightiest empire the world has yet seen," murmured Enid.

Soon they were home and gobbling up their dinner.

Enid inclined to the theory that imperialism of any sort was a self-defeating process, and she argued her case forcefully until Mrs. Brown sent them both off to bed.

"Good heavens," she said. "It won't be the first empire that's collapsed." And she tucked them up and snuffed out the candle. But secretly she was worried. What would replace the Roman hegemony? Would it mean a return to . . . she could hardly bring herself to think of it . . .

Mr. Brown returned home late that night. He had had a bad day at work. Someone had thrown a heavy object at him and broken four of his ribs, and he had caught his leg in a plow and severed it below the knee. As if that wasn't enough, he'd broken his nose sorting turnips, and his heart had stopped beating for three minutes. He flopped down in the chair, killing the cat.

"They're all talking about it down at the warren," he said, pulling off his boots.

"*What*, dear?" said Mrs. Brown innocently.

"You know . . . " he said impatiently, breaking one of his legs just below the knee, "the collapse of Roman imperialism."

"I know," admitted Mrs. Brown. "It worried me stiff when the children told me about it."

She put some butter on the table.

"Mmm . . . it's nice with butter," said Mr. Brown.

"I suppose," said Mrs. Brown, "that what with the collapse of Roman imperialism, it'll mean a return to—"

"Sssh!" said Mr. Brown, wrapping a tourniquet around his arm to stop the bleeding. "The children."

But Bill and Enid were wide awake in their beds, listening. What *did* the collapse of Roman imperialism mean for the ordinary Briton? What *was* it a return to . . . ?

They were still awake an hour later when Mr. Brown finished the table and came to bed, damaging his skull on the doorjamb.

## *Chapter Two: The Dark Stranger*

Bill, Enid, Johnny, Liz, and Paul were looking for birds' nests in Tadger's wood when suddenly Liz looked up and gave a little gasp.

There . . . staring her in the face was a lean young man with piercing blue eyes and a mane of flowing blond hair.

"Ik kaalhoved tak di gevinstsejre," he whispered.

From the little Danish that she knew, she recognized only "*kaalhoved*"—a cabbage—and "*gevinstsejre,*" meaning "prizewinning."

"Would you like to come and meet my friends?" she asked him cautiously.

He nodded.

It was only then that she noticed that he had an army with him. At first glance it looked to be around 9,000 strong, with bowmen in the front, spear carriers on the flank, and several thousand mounted cavalry in the rear. She pretended not to notice and led her new friend into the clearing where Johnny, Paul, Bill, and Enid were looking around anxiously for her.

"Hello!" said Enid. "Who's this?"

"Look out!" said Paul, noticing one of the spearmen idly running his spear through Kipper, the dog.

"Poor Kipper," said Enid.

In the massacre that followed, Mr. Brown was decapitated (twice), and Mr. Ottershaw from the pharmacy was sick (eight times). The children could hardly believe their eyes as many thousand of the infantry wiped out Mrs. Brown, the vicar who had just come to call, and all of the guinea pigs.

"Well!" said Enid. "This *is* a day!"

While they were burning the house to the ground, Bill and Johnny and Liz slipped away to see how things were back in Tadger's wood. There, sure enough, were piles of corpses: their parents and friends and all of the neighbors. Many had their ears cut off and ripped away and . . .

[This story has been discontinued by order of the publishers.]

# THE AFFAIR AT 7 RUE DE M—

## JOHN STEINBECK

I HAD HOPED to withhold from public scrutiny those rather curious events that had given me some concern for the past month. I knew, of course, that there was talk in the neighborhood; I have even heard some of the distortions current in my district—stories, I hasten to add, in which there is no particle of truth. However, my desire for privacy was shattered yesterday by a visit of two members of the fourth estate who assured me that the story or, rather, a story had escaped the boundaries of my arrondissement.

In the light of impending publicity, I think it only fair to issue the true details of those happenings that have come to be known as The Affair at 7 rue de M—, in order that nonsense may not be added to a set of circumstances that are not without their *bizarrerie*. I shall set down the events as they happened without comment, thereby allowing the public to judge the situation.

At the beginning of the summer, I carried my family to Paris and took up residence in a pretty little house at 7 rue de M—, a building that in another period had been the mews of the great house beside it. The whole property is now owned and part of it inhabited by a noble French family of such age and purity that its members still consider the Bourbons unacceptable as claimants to the throne of France.

To this pretty little converted stable with three floors of rooms, above a well-paved courtyard, I brought my immediate family, consisting of my wife, my three children (two small boys and a grown daughter), and, of course, myself. Our domestic arrangement in addition to the concierge, who, as you might say, came with the house, consists of a French cook of great ability, a Spanish maid, and my own secretary, a girl of Swiss nationality whose high attainments and ambitions are only equaled by her moral altitude. This, then, was our little family group when the events I am about to chronicle were ushered in.

If one must have an agency in this matter, I can find no alternative to placing not the blame, but rather the authorship, albeit innocent, on my younger son, John, who has only recently attained his eighth year, a lively child of singular beauty and buckteeth.

This young man has, during the last several years in America, become not so much an addict as an aficionado of that curious American practice, the chewing of bubblegum, and one of the pleasanter aspects of the early summer in Paris lay in the fact that the Cadet John had neglected to bring any of the atrocious substance with him from America. The child's speech became clear and unobstructed, and the hypnotized look went out of his eyes.

Alas, this delightful situation was not long to continue. An old family friend traveling in Europe brought as a present to the children a more than adequate supply of this beastly gum, thinking to do them a kindness. Thereupon the old familiar situation reasserted itself. Speech fought its damp way past a huge wad of the gum and emerged with the sound of a faulty water tap. The jaws were in constant motion, giving the face at best a look of agony, while the eyes took on a glaze like those of a pig with a recently severed jugular. Since I do not believe in inhibiting my children, I resigned myself to a summer not quite so pleasant as I had at first hoped.

On occasion I do not follow my ordinary practice of laissez faire. When I am composing the material for a book or play or essay, in a word, when the utmost of concentration is required, I am prone to establish tyrannical rules for my own comfort and effectiveness. One of these rules is that there shall be neither chewing nor bubbling while I am trying to concentrate. This rule is so thoroughly understood by the Cadet John that he accepts it as one of the laws of nature and does not either complain or attempt to evade the ruling. It is his pleasure and my solace for my son to come sometimes into my workroom, there to sit quietly beside me for a time. He knows that he must be silent, and when he has remained so for as long a time as his character permits, he goes out quietly, leaving us both enriched by the wordless association.

Two weeks ago in the late afternoon, I sat at my desk composing a short essay for *Figaro Littéraire*, an essay that later roused some controversy when it was printed under the title

"Sartre Resartus." I had come to that passage concerning the proper clothing for the soul, when, to my astonishment and chagrin, I heard the unmistakable soft plopping sound of a bursting balloon of bubblegum. I looked sternly at my offspring and saw him chewing away. His cheeks were colored with embarrassment, and the muscles of his jaws stood out rigidly.

"You know the rule," I said coldly.

To my amazement, tears came into his eyes, and while his jaws continued to masticate hugely, his blubbery voice forced its way past the huge lump of bubblegum in his mouth. "I didn't do it!"

"What do you mean, you didn't do it?" I demanded in a rage. "I distinctly heard, and now I distinctly see."

"Oh, sir!" he moaned. "I really didn't. I'm not chewing it, sir. It's chewing me."

For a moment I inspected him closely. He is an honest child, only under the greatest pressure of gain permitting himself an untruth. I had the horrible thought that the bubblegum had finally had its way and that my son's reason was tottering. If this was so, it were better to tread softly. Quietly, I put out my hand. "Lay it here," I said kindly.

My child manfully tried to disengage the gum from his jaws. "It won't let me go," he sputtered.

"Open up," I said, and then, inserting my fingers into his mouth, I seized hold of the large lump of gum and, after a struggle in which my fingers slipped again and again, managed to drag it forth and to deposit the ugly blob on my desk on top of a pile of white manuscript paper.

For a moment it seemed to shudder there on the paper and then with an easy slowness began to undulate, to swell and recede with the exact motion of being chewed while my son and I regarded it with popping eyes.

For a long time we watched it while I drove through my mind for some kind of explanation. Either I was dreaming, or some principle as yet unknown had taken its seat in the pulsing bubblegum on the desk. I am not unintelligent; while I considered the indecent thing, a hundred little thoughts and glimmerings of understanding raced through my brain. At last I asked, "How long has it been chewing you?"

"Since last night," he replied.

"And when did you first notice this, this propensity on its part?"

He spoke with perfect candor. "I will ask you to believe me, sir," he said. "Last night before I went to sleep I put it under my pillow, as is my invariable custom. In the night I was awakened to find that it was in my mouth. I again placed it under my pillow, and this morning it was again in my mouth, lying very quietly. When, however, I became thoroughly awakened, I was conscious of a slight motion, and shortly afterward the situation dawned on me that I was no longer the master of the gum. It had taken its head. I tried to remove it, sir, and could not. You yourself with all of your strength have seen how difficult it was to extract. I came to your study to wait till you were free, wishing to acquaint you with my difficulty. Oh, Daddy, what do you think has happened?"

The cancerous thing held my complete attention.

"I must think," I said. "This is something a little out of the ordinary, and I do not believe it should be passed over without some investigation."

As I spoke, a change came over the gum. It ceased to chew itself and seemed to rest for a while, and then with a flowing movement like those monocellular animals of the order paramecium, the gum slid across the desk straight in the direction of my son. For a moment I was stricken with astonishment, and for an even longer time I failed to discern its intent. It dropped to his knee and climbed horribly up his shirt front. Only then did I understand. It was trying to get back into his mouth. He looked down on it, paralyzed with fright.

"Stop," I cried, for I realized that my third-born was in danger, and at such times I am capable of a violence that verges on the murderous. I seized the monster from his chin and, striding from my study, entered the sitting room, opened the window, and hurled the thing into the busy traffic on the rue de M—.

I believe it is the duty of a parent to ward off those shocks that may cause dreams or trauma whenever possible. I went back to my study to find young John sitting where I had left him. He was staring into space. There was a troubled line between his brows.

"Son," I said, "you and I have seen something that, while we know it to have happened, we might find difficult to describe with any degree of success to others. I ask you to imagine the scene if we should tell this story to the other members of the family. I greatly fear we should be laughed out of the house."

"Yes, sir," he said passively.

"Therefore I am going to propose to you, my son, that we lock the episode deep in our memories and never mention it to a soul as long as we live." I waited for his assent and, when it did not come, glanced up at his face to see it a ravaged field of terror. His eyes were staring out of his head. I turned in the direction of his gaze; under the door there crept a paper-thin sheet that, once it had entered the room, grew to a gray blob and rested on the rug, pulsing and chewing. After a moment it moved again by pseudopodian progression toward my son.

I fought down panic as I rushed at it. I grabbed it up and flung it on my desk, and then, seizing an African war club from among the trophies on the wall, a dreadful instrument studded with brass, I beat the gum until I was breathless and it a torn piece of plastic fabric. The moment I rested, it drew itself together and for a few moments chewed very rapidly, as though it chuckled at my impotence, and then inexorably it moved toward my son, who by this time was crouched in a corner moaning with terror.

Now a coldness came over me. I picked up the filthy thing and wrapped it in my handkerchief, strode out of the house, walked three blocks to the Seine river and flung the handkerchief into the slowly moving current.

I spent a good part of the afternoon soothing my son and trying to reassure him that his fears were over. But such was his nervousness that I had to give him half a barbiturate tablet to get him to sleep that night, while my wife insisted that I call a doctor.

I did not at that time dare tell her why I could not obey her wish.

I was awakened, indeed the whole house was awakened, in the night by a terrified, muffled scream from the children's room. I took the stairs two at a time and burst into the room, flicking the light switch as I went. John sat up in bed squalling, while with his fingers he dug at his half-open mouth, a mouth that horrifyingly went right on chewing. As I looked, a bubble emerged between his fingers and burst with a wet plopping sound.

What chance of keeping our secret now! All had to be explained, but with the plopping gum pinned to a breadboard with an ice pick, the explanation was easier than it might have been. And I am proud of the help and comfort given to me. There is no strength like that of the family. Our French cook solved the problem by refusing to believe it even when she saw it. It was not reasonable, she explained, and she was a reasonable member of a reasonable people. The Spanish maid ordered and paid for an exorcism by the parish priest, who, poor man, after two hours of strenuous effort, went away muttering that this was more a matter of the stomach than of the soul.

For two weeks we were besieged by the monster. We burned it in the fireplace, causing it to splutter in blue flames and melt in a nasty mess among the ashes. Before morning it had crawled through the keyhole of the children's room, leaving a trail of wood ashes on the door, and again we were awakened by screams from the Cadet.

In despair I drove far into the country and threw it from my automobile. It was back before morning. Apparently it had crept to the highway and placed itself in the Paris traffic until picked up by a truck tire. When we tore it from John's mouth, it still had the nonskid marks of Michelin imprinted on its side.

Fatigue and frustration will take their toll. In exhaustion, with my will to fight back sapped, and after we had tried every possible method to lose or destroy the bubblegum, I placed it at last under a bell jar that I ordinarily use to cover my microscope. I collapsed in a chair to gaze at it with weary, defeated eyes. John slept in his little bed under the influence of sedatives, backed by my assurance that I would not let the Thing out of my sight.

I lighted a pipe and settled back to watch it. Inside the bell jar, the gray tumorous lump moved restlessly around searching for some means of exit from its prison. Now and then it paused as though in thought and emitted a bubble in my direction. I could feel the hatred that it had for me. In my weariness I found my mind slipping into an analysis that had so far escaped me.

The background I had been over hurriedly. It must be that from constant association with the lambent life that is my son, the magic life had been created inside the bubblegum. And with life had come intelligence, not the manly open intelligence of the boy, but an evil, calculating wiliness.

How could it be otherwise? Intelligence without the soul to balance it must of necessity be evil; the gum had not absorbed any part of John's soul.

Very well, said my mind, now that we have a hypothesis of its origin, let us consider its nature. What does it think? What does it want? What does it need? My mind leaped like a terrier. It needs and wants to get back to its host, my son. It wants to be chewed. It must be chewed in order to survive.

Inside the bell jar, the gum inserted a thin wedge of itself under the heavy glass foot and constricted so that the whole jar lifted a fraction of an inch. I laughed as I drove it back. I laughed with almost insane triumph. I had the answer.

In the dining room I procured a clear plastic plate, one of a dozen that my wife had bought for picnics in the country. Then turning the bell jar over and securing the monster in its bottom, I smeared the mouth of it with a heavy plastic cement guaranteed to be water-, alcohol- and acid-proof. I forced the plate over the opening and pressed it down until the glue took hold and bound the plate to the glass, making an airtight container. And last I turned the jar upright again and adjusted the reading light so that I could observe every movement of my prisoner.

Again it searched the circle for escape. Then it faced me and emitted a great number of bubbles very rapidly. I could hear the little bursting plops through the glass.

"I have you, my beauty," I cried. "I have you at last."

That was a week ago. I have not left the side of the bell jar since and have only turned my head to accept a cup of coffee. When I go to the bathroom, my wife takes my place. I can now report the following hopeful news.

During the first day and night, the bubblegum tried every means to escape. Then for a day and a night it seemed to be agitated and nervous, as though it had for the first time realized its predicament. The third day it went to work with its chewing motion, only the action was speeded up greatly, like the chewing of a baseball fan. On the fourth day it began to weaken, and I observed with joy a kind of dryness on its once slick and shiny exterior.

I am now in the seventh day, and I believe it is almost over. The gum is lying in the center of the plate. At intervals it heaves and subsides. Its color has turned to a nasty yellow. Once today, when my son entered the room, it leaped up excitedly and then seemed to realize its hopelessness and collapsed on the plate. It will die tonight, I think, and only then will I dig a deep hole in the garden, and I will deposit the sealed bell jar and cover it up and plant geraniums over it.

It is my hope that this account will set straight some of the silly tales that are being hawked in the neighborhood.

# A CHANGE OF AUNTS

VIVIEN ALCOCK

EVERYONE KNOWS THAT the pond in Teppit's wood is haunted. A young nursemaid once drowned herself there. She did it early one evening, with the sun sinking in the red sky and the smoke from the burning house drifting through the trees.

They say that she had slipped out to meet her sweetheart and left the two little children alone, with the fire blazing behind its guard in the nursery grate. Burned to cinders they were, the poor little ones, and the young nursemaid, insane with the guilt and grief of it, had done away with herself.

But she still can't rest, the tale goes; and at sunset, you'll see the smoke drifting through the trees, though a hundred years have passed since the big house burned down. Then, if you're wise, you'll run! For that's when the poor crazed ghost rises up, all wet from the dark pond, and goes seeking for the dead children. Searching and searching all through the woods for the little children ... *Take care she doesn't get you!*

Meg Thompson, who was 11, thought perhaps that she was too old to believe in ghosts. Her brother, William, believed in them,

157

but he was only eight. Aunt Janet seemed to, but perhaps she was only pretending, just to keep William company so that he need not feel ashamed.

Even in full daylight, Aunt Janet would hold their hands and run them past the pond, chanting the magic charm:

*"Lady of the little lake,*
*Come not nigh, for pity's sake!*
*Remember, when the sun is high,*
*We may safely pass you by."*

And they would race up the hill through the trees, until they arrived home, laughing, breathless, and safe.

They loved Aunt Janet, who had looked after them ever since their mother had died. Unfortunately, a neighbor's brother, who had come visiting from Australia, loved her too and carried her back to Adelaide as his bride.

That was when Aunt Gertrude came. She was as different from Aunt Janet as a hawk from a dove. Thin and hard and sharp, she seemed to wear her bones outside her skin and her eyes on stalks. She could see dirty fingernails through pockets, smuggled bedtime cats through blankets, and broken mugs through two layers of newspaper and a wastebasket lid.

"I'm up to all your tricks," she told them with a smile like stretched elastic.

She only smiled when their father was in the room. There were many things that she only did when he was there such as calling them her dears, and giving them cookies with their tea, and letting them watch television. Just as there were many things that she only did when their father was out such as feeding them on stale bread and margarine, slapping and punching them, and locking them in the cellar as a punishment.

They did not mind being shut in the cellar. They played soldiers with the bottles of wine or cricket with a lump of coal and a piece of wood. Or they sat on empty crates and planned vengeance on Aunt Gertrude.

"I'll get a gun and shoot her," William said. "I'll cut her up into little pieces with the carving knife and feed her to Tiddles."

"You'd only get sent to prison," Meg objected. "I'm going to write a letter to child welfare and tell them about her, and they'll put *her* in prison."

"They won't believe you," William said, "any more than Dad does."

Meg was silent.

"Why doesn't Dad believe us?" William asked.

"Because she's always nicer to us when he's here. Because she doesn't hit us hard enough to leave bruises. Because she's told him that we're liars." Meg hesitated and then added slowly, "And because he doesn't *want* to believe us."

"Why not?"

"She's our last aunt. If she went, he wouldn't know what to do with us. He might have to send us away, and that would be worse."

William looked doubtful, but before he could say anything, there was the sound of a door shutting upstairs.

"She's back! Look sad, William," Meg whispered. They did not want Aunt Gertrude to find out that they did not mind being locked in the cellar. She'd only think of another punishment. One that hurt.

"Meg," William whispered anxiously, "you haven't told her about the haunted pond, have you?"

Meg shook her head.

"She'd take me down there, I know she would. At sunset," William whispered, his eyes huge with fear. "At sunset, when it's dangerous to go."

"I won't let her," Meg said.

In September, their father had to go to Germany for a month on business. They both cried when he left, and this made Aunt Gertrude angry. As a punishment, she sent them to bed without supper, locking their rooms so that they could not sneak down at night to steal food from the kitchen.

"I'm up to all your little tricks," she told them.

They were so hungry the next day that they were almost glad that it was Wednesday. For, every Wednesday, Aunt Gertrude took them to have tea with a friend of hers who lived on Eggleston Street, three miles away by road and no buses. Mrs. Brown was as square as Aunt Gertrude was angular, but otherwise seemed to be made of the same material. Granite. But at least they got sandwiches and cake there and could close their ears to the insults that the two women aimed at them.

"The trouble I've had with them," Aunt Gertrude started off.

"I don't know what children are coming to, I'm sure," Mrs.

Brown agreed. And they went on and on until at last it was time to go.

The walk back was all uphill. Usually, Aunt Gertrude would stride ahead and shout at the children when they lagged behind. They never complained when their legs ached and blisters burst on their heels. They did not want Aunt Gertrude to find out about the shortcut through Teppit's wood. But this Wednesday, as they were getting ready to go, Aunt Gertrude said that she was tired.

"Looking after these two wears me out. I must tell John that he'll have to buy me a car. It's a long walk back up Eggleston Hill . . ."

"Up Eggleston Hill?" Mrs. Brown repeated, surprised. "Don't you take the shortcut through the woods?"

The children looked at each other in alarm.

"What shortcut?" Aunt Gertrude demanded. "I didn't know there was a shortcut. Nobody told me . . ." Her eyes looked around for someone to blame and found the children. "Did you know about the shortcut?" she asked angrily.

"Of course they knew. Everyone knows," Mrs. Brown said. She looked at Meg and William and smiled nastily. "Don't tell me that you're afraid to pass the haunted pond! I thought only babies were afraid of ghosts!" The sinking sun, shining through the window, flushed her face as if with wine. "Never mind," she said, her voice as falsely sweet as honey from a wasp, "I'm sure your dear Aunt Gertrude will cure you of such silly fancies."

William clutched hold of Meg's hand.

"I'm not going through the woods! I'm not! You can't make

us! Not at sunset!"

Meg put her arms around him. She could hear Mrs. Brown telling Aunt Gertrude about the ghost of the young nursemaid and Aunt Gertrude laughing scornfully.

"So you're frightened of ghosts, are you?" she said to the children after they had left the house. "You'd let your poor aunt walk two unnecessary miles because of some stupid old wives' tale. Your poor aunt who works so hard while you spend all day playing! I'll soon see about that."

She grabbed them each by a wrist with her hard fingers and dragged them down the path into the woods. The trees closed around them in a dark, whispering crowd, seeming to murmur, "The sun is setting . . . keep away, keep away!"

William began to struggle and kick. Aunt Gertrude let go of Meg and hit William so hard that he was knocked right off the path. He fell into a deep drift of dead leaves that rose up like brown butterflies and settled down on him as he lay whimpering.

Meg ran to comfort him. "You'll have a bruise," she whispered softly. "You'll have a big bruise to show Dad when he comes back."

He smiled through his tears.

"What's that? What are you two plotting?" Aunt Gertrude asked sharply. "Any more nonsense out of you, and there's plenty more where that came from. Well? Are you going to behave?"

She stood over them, as tall and thin and hard as an iron lamppost, with the setting sun seeming to glow redly in her hateful eyes.

"Meg," William whispered, his arms around her neck, "I think she's a witch. Don't you? Meg, d'you think she's a witch?"

"No," Meg whispered back, more decidedly than she felt. "Come on, we'd better do what she says. Don't be frightened. I'll look after you, William."

So they walked down into the sighing woods. Their aunt marched behind them, throwing a long shadow that struck at their feet. William held tight to Meg's hand, and as soon as the dark pond came into sight, they began to chant under their breath the words of the magic charm:

> "*Lady of the little lake,*
> *Come not nigh, for pity's sake!*
> *Remember, when the sun is high . . .*"

"What are you two whispering about?" Aunt Gertrude demanded.

"Nothing," they answered.

For it was no good, the magic charm. It only worked in daylight, when the sun was up. Now the sun had fallen into the trees, and the sky was on fire.

"Look!" William whispered.

Between the trees, pale wisps of smoke came curling and creeping over the ground, like blind fingers searching . . .

"It's the smoke! Meg, it's the smoke!" William screamed.

Aunt Gertrude grabbed his shoulder and shook him.

"Stop that din! Making an exhibition of yourself! It's only mist rising from the water. Come, I'll show you." She started dragging

William toward the pond. Meg grabbed him by the other arm, and for a moment they pulled him between them, like a wishbone. Then Aunt Gertrude hit Meg hard on the ear, and Meg let go, putting her hands to her ringing head.

Aunt Gertrude forced William to the very edge of the dark pond.

"There! Look down—there's nothing there, is there, you stupid little coward? Answer me! There's nothing there, is there?"

She was looking at William as she spoke. She did not see what both the children saw. She did not see what rose out of the pond behind her.

It was something dark and wet, a figure of water and weeds. Green mud clung like flesh to its washed bones. A frog crouched like a pumping heart in its cage of ivory. Its crazed eyes, as silver as the scales of fish, glared down at Aunt Gertrude as she hit the terrified boy. It reached out . . .

Aunt Gertrude screamed.

William pulled away from her and ran. Blind with fear, he raced past Meg without seeing her and disappeared into the trees.

Meg could not move. She crouched down on the damp, leafy ground and watched in terror. Dark water was torn from the pond in creamy tatters as the two figures struggled together, the screaming aunt and the other one, all water and weeds and bones. Its silver eyes glinting, it fastened its ivory fingers like combs into Aunt Gertrude's hair. Down, down they sank in a boil of bubbles.

"Meg! Meg!" William's voice called from among the trees, and Meg, as if released, leaped to her feet and ran after him, leaving Aunt Gertrude in the pond.

William had fallen over. His knee was bleeding, his bruised face wet.

"Come on, come on, hurry!" Meg said, catching hold of his hand and dragging him after her.

For there was someone following. Running through the trees behind them, twigs snapping, leaves crunching under invisible feet.

"Run, William, faster, faster!" Meg cried.

"I can't!"

"You must! Run, William, run!"

It was closer now, and closer, following fast, bounding in huge leaps over the rotting branches and white nests of toadstools.

"Faster!" Meg cried, looking fearfully over her shoulder at the shaking bushes, not seeing the twisted root that caught at her feet. She fell, bringing William down with her.

Aunt Gertrude burst through the bushes.

How strange she looked! She had run so fast that the clothes had dried on her body, and her cheeks were pink. Her hair, loosened from its tight knot, was tumbled and tangled all over her head.

The children cowered away from her as she came up and knelt down beside them.

"Are you all right, my little dears?" she asked softly. (*Dears?*) "That was a nasty tumble! Why, you're shivering, Miss Margaret! And Master William, you've cut your poor knee." (*Miss? Master?*) "If you're a brave boy and don't cry, I'll give you a piggyback ride home, and there'll be hot chocolate and cherry cake by the nursery fire."

They stared at her, trembling. The look in Aunt Gertrude's eyes was soft and kind. The smile on Aunt Gertrude's mouth was wide and sweet. What was she up to? What cruel trick was she playing now?

They were silent as Aunt Gertrude carried William up the hill to their home. There, as good as her word, she gave them hot chocolate and cake and sat them on the sofa while she bathed William's knee.

When she had finished, she stood up and gazed at the empty grate in the living room, while they watched her silently. Then she left the room. They sipped their hot chocolate, sitting side by side, listening. They could hear her going from room to room all over the house, as if looking for something.

"What's she up to?" William whispered.

"I don't know."

"Did you see it? Did you see it . . . in the pond?"

"Yes."

"What happened, Meg?"

"Aunt Gertrude fell in," Meg said and shivered.

"Why is she so . . . so different?"

"I don't know."

"I wish Daddy was back," William said, and his lip quivered. Meg put her arm around him, and they were silent again, listening to the footsteps going around and around the house, slowly, uncertainly, as if Aunt Gertrude had lost her way.

★★★

There was no doubt that Aunt Gertrude was a changed woman since she had fallen into the pond. Perhaps the water had washed the nastiness out of her. The house had never been so bright and cheerful. Their meals had never been so delicious. She made them apple pie and cherry cake and let them lick out the bowls. She played leapfrog with them in the garden and never minded running after the balls in cricket. She told them bedtime stories and kissed them good night.

William started calling her Aunt Trudie and would often hold her hand, taking her to see some treasure—a large snail with a whirligig shell, a stone with a hole right through the middle, or a jay's feather. Meg followed them silently, watching and listening. Once, when William did not know that she was behind them, she heard him say, "Aunt Trudie, you mustn't call us Miss Margaret and Master William, you know."

"Should I not, Master William?"

"No. Just plain Meg and William."

"William, then."

"That's better. And when Daddy comes home on Saturday, you must call him John. Can you remember that?"

She smiled and nodded.

"Don't worry," he said. "I'll look after you, Aunt Trudie." Then he caught sight of Meg behind them and said quickly, "We're just playing a game. Go away, Meg! We don't want you!"

"Now, Mas . . . Now, William, that's no way to speak to your sister," Aunt Trudie said gently. "Of course we want her." She smiled at Meg. "We are going to see the kittens next door. Come with us, Meg."

Meg shook her head and walked back to the house. She went up to Aunt Gertrude's bedroom and looked around. It was bright and clean, and there were flowers on the dressing table. There was no smell, no sense of Aunt Gertrude in it anywhere. It seemed like another person's room. Meg sat down on the bed and thought for a long time.

Aunt Trudie found her there when she came in from the garden, flushed and laughing. She hesitated when she caught sight of Meg and then called over her shoulder, "Just a moment, William! Wait for me in the garden."

Then she shut the door and leaned against it, looking gravely and kindly at Meg.

"Will you be staying with us long?" Meg asked politely.

"As long as ever you want me to," was the answer.

There was a short silence. Then Meg jumped to her feet and put her arms around the woman.

"We don't want you to go, Aunt Trudie," she said. "We want you to stay with us forever."


It was three years before Meg ventured once more into Teppit's wood. She went in broad daylight, when the sun was high. It was curiosity that took her there, down the winding path to the dark pond at the bottom. It was a warm day, and birds were singing in the trees. The pond looked peaceful. There was frog's spawn in the brown water, leaves floated on the surface like little islands, and a water boatman sculled across, leaving a silver wake behind it.

Meg stood a safe distance away and waited.

Bubbles began to disturb the quiet water. Small fish darted away and hid under the weeds. Now a scum of mud and filth rose slowly up from the bottom of the pond. It spread around a clump of frog's spawn, which shook and seemed to separate and then reform into the shape of a hideous, scowling face.

As she watched, Meg thought that she heard, faintly, a familiar voice.

"Meg! Get me out! Get me out this minute! She's stolen my body, that wretched servant girl! Meg, if you bring her down here, I'll give you a penny. I'll give you chocolate cookies every day. And roast beef! Just bring her down here and push her in! Meg, I'll never hit you again, I promise, I promise, promise . . ."

"Goodbye, Aunt Gertrude," Meg said firmly and left. That was the last time she ever walked in the woods around Teppit's pond.

# THE CASK OF AMONTILLADO

EDGAR ALLAN POE

THE THOUSAND INJURIES of Fortunato I had borne as I best could; but when he ventured upon insult, I vowed revenge. You, who so well know the nature of my soul, will not suppose, however, that I gave utterance to a threat. At length I would be avenged; this was a point definitely settled—but the very definitiveness with which it was resolved precluded the idea of risk. I must not only punish, but punish with impunity. A wrong is unredressed when retribution overtakes its redresser. It is equally unredressed when the avenger fails to make himself felt as such to him who has done the wrong.

It must be understood that neither by word nor deed had I given Fortunato cause to doubt my goodwill. I continued, as was my wont, to smile in his face, and he did not perceive that my smile *now* was at the thought of his immolation.

He had a weak point—this Fortunato—although in other regards he was a man to be respected and even feared. He prided himself on his connoisseurship in wine. Few Italians have the true virtuoso spirit. For the most part their enthusiasm is adapted to suit the time and opportunity—to practice imposture upon the

British and Austrian millionaires. In painting and gemology, Fortunato, like his countrymen, was a quack—but in the matter of wines, he was sincere. In this respect I did not differ from him materially; I was skillful in the Italian vintages myself and bought largely whenever I could.

It was around dusk, one evening during the supreme madness of the carnival season, that I encountered my friend. He accosted me with excessive warmth, for he had been drinking much. The man wore motley. He had on a tight-fitting parti-striped dress, and his head was surmounted by the conical cap and bells. I was so pleased to see him that I thought I should never have done wringing his hand.

I said to him, "My dear Fortunato, you are luckily met. How remarkably well you are looking today! But I have received a pipe of what passes for amontillado, and I have my doubts."

"How?" said he. "Amontillado? A pipe? Impossible! And in the middle of the carnival!"

"I have my doubts," I replied; "and I was silly enough to pay the full amontillado price without consulting you in the matter. You were not to be found, and I was fearful of losing a bargain."

"Amontillado!"

"I have my doubts."

"Amontillado!"

"And I must satisfy them."

"Amontillado!"

"As you are engaged, I am on my way to Luchesi. If anyone

has a critical turn, it is he. He will tell me—"

"Luchesi can not tell amontillado from sherry."

"And yet some fools will have it that his taste is a match for your own."

"Come, let us go."

"Whither?"

"To your vaults."

"My friend, no; I will not impose upon your good nature. I perceive you have an engagement. Luchesi—"

"I have no engagement; come."

"My friend, no. It is not the engagement, but the severe cold with which I perceive you are afflicted. The vaults are insufferably damp. They are encrusted with niter."

"Let us go, nevertheless. The cold is merely nothing. Amontillado! You have been imposed upon. And as for Luchesi, he can not distinguish sherry from amontillado."

Thus speaking, Fortunato possessed himself of my arm. Putting on a mask of black silk and drawing a roquelaure closely around my person, I suffered him to hurry me to my palazzo.

There were no attendants at home; they had absconded to make merry in honor of the time. I had told them that I should not return until the morning and had given them explicit orders not to stir from the house. These orders were sufficient, I well knew, to insure their immediate disappearance, one and all, as soon as my back was turned.

I took from their sconces two flambeaux and, giving one to Fortunato, bowed him through several suites of rooms to the archway that led into the vaults. I passed down a long and winding staircase, requesting him to be cautious as he followed. We came at length to the foot of the descent and stood together on the damp ground of the catacombs of the Montresors.

The gait of my friend was unsteady, and the bells upon his cap jingled as he strode.

"The pipe?" said he.

"It is further on," said I; "but observe the white web work that gleams from these cavern walls."

He turned toward me and looked into my eyes with two filmy orbs that distilled the rheum of intoxication.

"Niter?" he asked at length.

"Niter," I replied. "How long have you had that cough?"

"Ugh! ugh! ugh!—ugh! ugh! ugh!—ugh! ugh! ugh!—ugh! ugh! ugh!—ugh! ugh! ugh!"

My poor friend found it impossible to reply for many minutes.

"It is nothing," he said at last.

"Come," I said with decision, "we will go back; your health is precious. You are rich, respected, admired, beloved; you are happy, as once I was. You are a man to be missed. For me it is no matter. We will go back; you will be ill, and I cannot be responsible. Besides, there is Luchesi—"

"Enough," he said; "the cough is a mere nothing; it will not kill me. I shall not die of a cough."

"True—true," I replied; "and, indeed, I had no intention of alarming you unnecessarily; but you should use all proper caution.

A draft of this Medoc will defend us from the damp."

Here I knocked off the neck of a bottle that I drew from a long row of its fellows that lay upon the mold.

"Drink," I said, presenting him the wine.

He raised it to his lips with a leer. He paused and nodded to me familiarly, while his bells jingled.

"I drink," he said, "to the buried that repose around us."

"And I to your long life."

He again took my arm, and we proceeded.

"These vaults," he said, "are extensive."

"The Montresors," I replied, "were a great and numerous family."

"I forget your arms."

"A huge human foot d'or in a field azure; the foot crushes a serpent rampant whose fangs are embedded in the heel."

"And the motto?"

"*Nemo me impune lacessit.*"

"Good!" he said.

The wine sparkled in his eyes, and the bells jingled. My own fancy grew warm with the Medoc. We had passed through walls of piled bones, with casks and puncheons intermingling, into the inmost recesses of the catacombs. I paused again, and this time I made bold to seize Fortunato by an arm above the elbow.

"The niter!" I said. "See, it increases. It hangs like moss upon the vaults. We are below the river's bed. The drops of moisture trickle among the bones. Come, we will go back ere it is too late. Your cough—"

"It is nothing," he said; "let us go on. But first, another draft of the Medoc."

I broke and reached him a flagon of De Grâve. He emptied it at a breath. His eyes flashed with a fierce light. He laughed and threw the bottle upward with a gesticulation that I did not understand.

I looked at him in surprise. He repeated the movement—a grotesque one.

"You do not comprehend?" he said.

"Not I," I replied.

"Then you are not of the brotherhood."

"How?"

"You are not of the masons?"

"Yes, yes," I said; "yes, yes."

"You? Impossible! A mason?"

"A mason," I replied.

"A sign," he said.

"It is this," I answered, producing a trowel from beneath the folds of my roquelaure.

"You jest," he exclaimed, recoiling a few paces. "But let us proceed to the amontillado."

"Be it so," I said, replacing the tool beneath the cloak and again offering him my arm. He leaned upon it heavily. We continued our route in search of the amontillado. We passed through a range of low arches, descended, passed on, and, descending again, arrived at a deep crypt in which the foulness of the air caused our flambeaux rather to glow than flame.

At the most remote end of the crypt there appeared another less spacious. Its walls had been lined with human remains, piled to the vault overhead in the fashion of the great catacombs of Paris. Three sides of this interior crypt were still ornamented in this manner. From the fourth the bones had been thrown down and lay promiscuously upon the earth, forming at one point a mound of some size. Within the wall thus exposed by the displacing of the bones we perceived a still interior recess, in depth around four feet, in width three, in height six or seven. It seemed to have been constructed for no especial use within itself, but formed merely the interval between two of the colossal supports of the roof of the catacombs and was backed by one of their circumscribing walls of solid granite.

It was in vain that Fortunato, uplifting his dull torch, endeavored to pry into the depth of the recess. Its termination the feeble light did not enable us to see.

"Proceed," I said; "herein is the amontillado. As for Luches—"

"He is an ignoramus," interrupted my friend as he stepped unsteadily forward, while I followed immediately at his heels. In an instant he had reached the extremity of the niche and, finding his progress arrested by the rock, stood stupidly bewildered. A moment more, and I had fettered him to the granite. In its surface were two iron staples, distant from each other around two feet horizontally. From one of these depended a short chain; from the other, a padlock. Throwing the links around his waist, it was but the work of a few seconds to secure it. He was too much astounded to resist. Withdrawing the key, I stepped back from the recess.

"Pass your hand," I said, "over the wall; you cannot help feeling the niter. Indeed, it is *very* damp. Once more let me *implore* you to return. No? Then I must positively leave you. But I must first render you all of the little attentions in my power."

"The amontillado!" ejaculated my friend, not yet recovered from his astonishment.

"True," I replied; "the amontillado."

As I said these words, I busied myself among the pile of bones of which I have before spoken. Throwing them aside, I soon uncovered a quantity of building stone and mortar. With these materials and with the aid of my trowel, I began vigorously to wall up the entrance of the niche.

I had scarcely laid the first tier of the masonry when I discovered that the intoxication of Fortunato had in a great measure worn off. The earliest indication I had of this was a low moaning cry from the depth of the recess. It was not the cry of a drunken man. There was then a long and obstinate silence. I laid the second tier, and the third, and the fourth; and then I heard the furious vibrations of the chain. The noise lasted for several minutes, during which, that I might hearken to it with the more satisfaction, I ceased my labor and sat down upon the bones. When at last the clanking subsided, I resumed the trowel and finished without interruption the fifth, the sixth, and the seventh tier. The wall was now almost upon a level with my breast. I again paused and, holding the flambeaux over the masonry, threw a few feeble rays upon the figure within.

A succession of loud and shrill screams, bursting suddenly from the throat of the chained form, seemed to thrust me violently back. For a brief moment I hesitated—I trembled. Unsheathing my rapier, I began to grope with it around the recess; but the thought of an instant reassured me. I placed my hand upon the solid fabric of the catacombs and felt satisfied. I reapproached the wall. I replied to the yells of him who clamored. I reechoed—I aided—I surpassed them in volume and in strength. I did this, and the clamorer grew still.

It was now midnight, and my task was drawing to a close. I had completed the eighth, the ninth, and the tenth tier. I had finished a portion of the last and the 11th; there remained but a single stone to be fitted and plastered in. I struggled with its weight; I placed it partially in its destined position. But now there came from out of the niche a low laugh that erected the hairs upon my head. It was succeeded by a sad voice, which I had difficulty in recognizing as that of the noble Fortunato. The voice said, "Ha! ha! ha!—he! he!—a very good joke indeed—an excellent jest. We will have many a rich laugh about it at the palazzo—he! he! he!—over our wine—he! he! he!"

"The amontillado!" I said.

"He! he! he!—he! he! he!—yes, the amontillado. But is it not getting late? Will not they be awaiting us at the palazzo, the Lady Fortunato and the rest? Let us be gone."

"Yes," I said, "let us be gone."

"*For the love of God, Montresor!*"

"Yes," I said, "for the love of God!"

But to these words I hearkened in vain for a reply. I grew impatient. I called aloud, "Fortunato!"

No answer. I called again, "Fortunato!"

No answer still. I thrust a torch through the remaining aperture and let it fall within. There came forth in return only a jingling of the bells. My heart grew sick—on account of the dampness of the catacombs. I hastened to make an end of my labor. I forced the last stone into its position; I plastered it up. Against the new masonry I reerected the old rampart of bones. For the half of a century no mortal has disturbed them. *In pace requiescat!*

# THE PEAR DRUM

## ENGLISH FOLKTALE

ONCE UPON A time there were two little girls. Their names were Blue Eyes and Turkey. Blue Eyes was named after the color of her eyes and Turkey after the red dress that she wore. They lived in a little house on a moor with their mother and the baby. Their father was a sailor voyaging to faraway lands.

One day Blue Eyes and Turkey went for a walk upon the moor, and they met a gypsy girl playing on a pear drum. When she played, a little man and woman came out of the drum and danced. Blue Eyes and Turkey were enchanted and begged her to give them the pear drum. "I will give it you," she said, "but only if you are very naughty! Come back tomorrow."

So, Blue Eyes and Turkey were very naughty. They shouted, and spilled their food, and refused to go to bed, and scribbled on their books. Their mother was grieved, but the next day they got up very early and went out on the moor. There they met the gypsy girl, and again she played the pear drum. "We were very naughty," they cried. "Can we have it?" "Tell me what you did," she replied. So they told her. "Oh, no," said the gypsy girl, "you were only a little naughty. You must be much worse than that."

So that day they were as naughty as they could be. They threw their cups on the floor, and tore their clothes, and walked in mud up to their knees; and pulled up all of the flowers in the garden, and let out the pig so that it ran away. Their mother was still more grieved than before, but the next day they got up very early and went out to meet the gypsy girl. Again she told them that they had not been naughty enough. "You must be really bad," she said.

So they went home. This time they broke the chairs and smashed the china, and tore their clothes to pieces, and whipped the dog, and struck the baby, and beat their mother with their fists. Their mother said sadly, "Blue Eyes and Turkey, you must not be so naughty. If you do not stop, I shall have to go away, and instead there will come a new mother with glass eyes and a wooden tail to live with you." But still they thought of the wonderful pear drum and said to each other, "Tomorrow we will be good. Once we have the pear drum, we will be good again."

The next morning they got up very early and went out on the moor. There was the gypsy girl, but she had no pear drum. "Where is the pear drum?" they cried. The gypsy girl laughed. "It is gone. We gypsies are all going away today. I am the last to leave." "But we did as you told us"—and they told her all the things that they had done. The gypsy girl laughed again. "Yes," she said, "you have been *really* naughty, and now your mother has gone away, far, far away to find your father, and instead you have a mother with glass eyes and a wooden tail."

Blue Eyes and Turkey wandered around on the moor all day, but when evening came, they went back to their house. There were no lamps lit, but in the glow of the firelight they could see through the window the glitter of their new mother's glass eyes and hear the thump of her wooden tail.

# THE DOG GOT THEM

PHILIPPA PEARCE

WHEN CAPTAIN JOEL Jones retired from the sea, he was persuaded by his wife to buy a handy little bungalow in the middle of nowhere in particular. Here the two of them lived very quietly—but with a certain amount of mystery. At least, to Andy Potter, their grandnephew, there was mystery.

Andy knew Aunt Enid fairly well—really, she was Great-Aunt Enid, of course; she used to visit her relations while the Captain was at sea. She was kind, but very prim. She liked to help with the washing up, mending of clothes, ironing—anything; but she and the Captain had had no children, and she exclaimed a good deal at the noisiness of Andy's friends and the language that young people used nowadays.

Captain Joel was another matter altogether. Andy had met him only rarely, on his return from voyages: a big, red-faced, restless man with a loud voice. (Andy's mother complained privately about *his* language.) When he drank tea, he picked up and set down the cup with a good deal of rattling of china against china. In excuse, he said that he was rather unfamiliar with tea as a beverage. He liked to carry Andy's father off for an evening at the

pub. He was always sociable and said that the Potters must all
come and stay in the new bungalow when they had moved in.
There would be two bedrooms: he and Aunt Enid would use
one, of course, but Andy's parents could have the other, and Andy
himself, still being a little boy, could sleep on the sofa in the sitting
room. Andy could even bring his terrier puppy, Teaser, if he was
careful about the Joneses' cat.

They moved in; but, oddly, the invitation to the Potters was
never renewed.

Mrs. Potter said, "It's not as if I particularly *want* to stay; but all
the same I wonder why they don't press us to go. Aunt Enid's so
often stayed here; and the Captain, too—and I could have done
without the smell of whiskey in the bedroom cupboard
afterward."

Mr. Potter said, "It'll take some time for them to settle down.
Especially for Joel: no sea, no shipmates, no pub near, no
company of any kind except Aunt Enid's."

"You make it sound like a bad move for them."

"Well . . ."

Andy listened, without paying much attention.

Over a year later, on their way back from a holiday by car, the
Potters found that they would be passing quite close to the new
bungalow. They decided to drop in—and not to telephone ahead
about the visit in case, as Mrs. Potter said, the answer was, Not
at home.

They parked the car outside the bungalow, and all got out—

all except Teaser. He was left in the car, chiefly because of the Joneses' old tabby. In a harmless way, Teaser was always on the lookout for cats. He loved any chase—no doubt, would have loved any fight, too. He came from a breed once specialist in ratting.

They rang the doorbell. From inside they could hear some exclamation of dismay (was it Aunt Enid's voice?) and a much louder, violent exclamation, undoubtedly in the Captain's voice. There was the sound of light footsteps, and the front door was opened.

"Oh, dear!" cried Aunt Enid on seeing them. "Oh, dear, oh, dear! How very nice to see you all!"

She did not move from the doorway.

Mrs. Potter said, "We were just passing, Aunt Enid. We thought we'd call to see how you'd settled in. Just a very brief visit." As Aunt Enid said nothing, Mrs. Potter added for her, "Just time for a quick cup of tea, perhaps, and a chat." "Of course!" said Aunt Enid. "How very nice! But it's not at all suitable, I'm afraid. The Captain is in bed with influenza. Severe influenza."

There was a roar from inside the bungalow: "Enid! I say, Enid!"

"There's my patient calling!" cried Aunt Enid. "Perhaps another time, when he's stronger . . . but telephone first." To everyone's astonishment, she began to close the door.

Mr. Potter put his foot in the doorway. "Aunt Enid," he said, "we don't want to come where we're not wanted for any reason; but—you're all right, aren't you?"

"Oh, perfectly, perfectly!" cried Aunt Enid. "I'm perfectly all right, and so is the Captain. He is in perfect health. It's just that, with infection in the house, I simply cannot—*cannot*—risk having visitors. I admit only the doctor, ever." She stooped and put her hands around Mr. Potter's leg to lift it from the doorway. He withdrew it to save her the trouble.

Aunt Enid was in the act of shutting the front door. Mrs. Potter said quickly, "Aunt Enid, promise to let us know at once if we can help you at any time, in any way."

Aunt Enid's face still showed in the gap of the doorway. Her eyes filled with tears. "My dear, you are truly kind," she said. Then, "But no help is required. I have the Captain, you know." This time she finished shutting the front door. They heard her "goodbye" from the other side.

They went back to the car in silence. As they were driving off, Andy's mother said, "She looked so worried and miserable. It couldn't be just the Captain's flu."

"She didn't even seem certain that he *was* ill," said Andy's father.

And Andy said, "He wasn't in bed. I looked past Aunt Enid when you were talking. I saw him. He wasn't even in pajamas."

"What was he doing?"

"Just walking around, in a wandering sort of way. Waving something in the air."

"Waving what?"

"I think it was a bottle."

Later, when they got home, Mrs. Potter wrote to Aunt Enid,

and then she began writing regularly, once every two weeks. Occasionally she had a reply. She would pass it to Andy's father to read, but never read it aloud to them all. Andy wondered.

Then, after many months, Aunt Enid wrote to say that Captain Joel had died.

"What did he die of?" asked Andy.

His parents looked at him thoughtfully, sizing him up, Andy knew: was he old enough to be told whatever it was?

"Yes," said his mother, "you're old enough to know; and it should be a warning to you all of your life: Captain Joel drank."

"So does Dad," said Andy. "You mean, more than that?"

"He drank much more," said his father. "He drank much, much too much. He died of it."

"Oh," said Andy. There was a mystery gone, it seemed.

After the funeral, which Mr. and Mrs. Potter attended, Aunt Enid came to stay for a bit. She was pale, thin, and apt to burst into tears for no clear reason. Andy's mother gave her breakfast in bed during her stay and would not let her help as much as usual with the housework. She had long private talks with her, after which they both seemed to have been crying.

"Poor woman," said Andy's mother, when Aunt Enid had gone. "It was a perfectly dreadful time when the Captain was dying. Appalling."

"DTs?" asked Andy's father.

His mother nodded.

Andy asked what DTs were.

"*Delirium tremens*," said his mother. "A particularly awful kind of deliriousness, from drinking too much for too long. You see things. It's a waking nightmare, according to Aunt Enid." She shuddered. "Horrible."

In due course a letter arrived from Aunt Enid thanking them all for her stay and saying that she felt much better as a result. She had the energy now to start getting the house right again after the Captain's death. She had already changed his sickroom back into a spare room. "But," she said, "I'm not sure that they've faded yet."

"They?" Andy's mother queried, passing the letter to her husband.

"Mistake for *it*, I suppose," said Mr. Potter, studying the letter. "*It* being the smell of booze or something like that."

"Her letter says *they* quite clearly," said Andy, also looking.

"Makes no sense," said his father; and the subject was dropped.

In the next letter Aunt Enid was very much upset because the cat had died. The cat had grown very old and poor in health; but, mysteriously, Aunt Enid seemed to blame herself for its death. She said that it had had a shock that she ought to have been able to spare it, and she thought that this shock had caused its death. She had not closely enough supervised where the cat had gone in the house—"But you don't supervise where a cat goes around indoors, to spare it shock," said Andy's father.

The next letter was written from the hospital. Aunt Enid had fallen and broken her hip, running too fast on the polished floors in the bungalow. She explained briefly: "I was afraid of not getting the door shut in time."

"Why should she be running to *shut doors in time*?" Andy's father asked crossly. He foresaw upheavals, if Aunt Enid was in the hospital.

He was right. Mrs. Potter telephoned the hospital to suggest a visit; and they had an express letter from Aunt Enid to say that she was looking forward to seeing them on the weekend and suggesting that they stay overnight in the bungalow. Andy's father and mother could sleep in the double bed in Aunt Enid's room; Andy himself could sleep on the sofa in the sitting room. If they had to bring Teaser, she did not advise that he came indoors at all: could he not sleep in the car and be exercised from there? She was sorry that the spare room was not yet habitable; she did not think that they had faded yet. The key to the bungalow would be in the milk box by the back door.

"This fading," said Andy's father, "*what is she talking about?*" He was exasperated. However, he agreed that they should all go down, as Aunt Enid had suggested, and they did.

The bungalow was neat and clean, as one would have expected of Aunt Enid's home; but it seemed empty and lifeless, with even the cat dead. They decided to leave Teaser mostly in the car, as Aunt Enid had wished it. Andy's parents would sleep in Aunt Enid's own room; but what about Andy? It was all very well for Aunt Enid to suggest the sofa: she had forgotten how time had passed—how much older Andy was, how much bigger. So they discussed the suitability of Aunt Enid's spare room, after all.

Standing in the spare room, looking around, they could see nothing against its use. Like the rest of the bungalow, it was neat and clean, with a single bed and a bedside lamp that worked. The room had no special features. There was a chiming clock on the mantelpiece—at least, Andy's mother said that it used to chime, but it had stopped working altogether by now. (Andy tried to wind it, in vain.) There was a cactus in a pot on the windowsill and a white china rabbit heading a procession of little white china rabbits on a dressing table.

"Why didn't she want us to use the room?" Andy's mother asked suspiciously. They had a good look around. Nothing odd and absolutely no trace left of the late Captain Joel, except for an empty whiskey bottle that Andy spotted, poking up the chimney.

Andy decided for himself by unrolling his sleeping bag on the single bed.

After supper, they all went to bed.

Andy woke up in what seemed like the middle of the night, but the room was not really dark. He thought that he had been woken by a noise: a squeaking, perhaps. Now he was almost sure that there was a soft scrabbling sound from the floor beyond the bottom of the bed. Very quietly he raised himself on his elbow to look. Against the far wall, heads together as if conferring, were two rats. They must be rats, and yet they were much, much larger than any ordinary rat, and their color was a gray white splotched with chestnut brown. He disliked their coloring very much. They seemed to have heard the slight creak of Andy's bedsprings, for now they turned their heads to look at him. They had pink eyes.

Then they began creeping to and fro against the wall and then running, in an agitated kind of way, almost as if they were getting up their courage. Each time they ran in the direction of the bed, they ran closer than they had done the last time. Especially the bigger of the two rats, which Andy assumed to be the male. The female lagged behind a little, always; but still she ran a little closer to the bed every time.

The male rat was scurrying closer and closer, and suddenly the knowledge came to Andy that it was going to attack. He was appalled. Frantically, he prepared to ward off its attack with his naked hand. The rat sprang, launching its heavy body through the air like a missile, and sank its teeth into his hand.

Andy was already on his feet on the bed. He knew that the female rat would attack next. The male hung from his hand as he slapped it violently, madly, repeatedly against the wall so that the body of the iron-teethed monster banged again and again and again against the wall. It seemed to him that almost simultaneously the body of the rat suddenly flew from its head, teeth still clenched in his flesh, and he himself flew from the dreadful bedroom. He slammed the door behind him against the female rat and rushed into his parents' room. They had already turned on the light, roused by his screaming.

Andy was still screaming, "Look! The rat—the rat!" He held out his hand for them to see the horror hanging from it.

They all looked at his hand: Andy's brown right hand, just as it always had been, entirely unmarked except where he had once scarred himself with a saw long ago. No rat.

"You've been dreaming," said his mother. "You were asleep, and you had a nightmare."

"No," said Andy, "I was awake." And he told them everything.

They went back into the spare room with him. There were no rats of course, nor any sign of one.

Staring around, Andy's father said at last, "They weren't your rats, Andy; they were the Captain's. And, as your great-aunt said, they haven't faded yet."

They shut the door fast on the spare room and made up a bed of sorts for Andy in the sitting room, with pillows on the floor and then his sleeping bag on top. Then they all went back to bed.

But—not surprisingly, perhaps—Andy could not get to sleep. He found that he was listening for sounds behind the door of the spare room. In the end he got up quietly and went out of the bungalow and brought Teaser in from the car for company. Teaser was delighted.

Andy had begun to fall asleep with the comforting weight of Teaser on his feet, when the dog left him. He was slipping out of the sitting room, whose door had been deliberately left ajar; Andy called softly, but Teaser paid no attention. Andy got up and followed him. But now Teaser was across the hall and at the spare room door. His nose was at the bottom crack, moving to and fro along it, sampling the air there. His tail moved occasionally, stiffly, in pleasure or in pleasurable anticipation.

Andy thought that he heard a squeak from the other side of the door: *two* squeaks—the squeaks of two different rat voices.

"No, Teaser," whispered Andy. "Oh, no!"

But Teaser looked over his shoulder at Andy, and his look spoke. On impulse Andy opened the spare room door a few inches, and at once Teaser had pushed past it into the room.

Instantly there was tumult—a wild barking, and the rush of scuttering feet, and objects falling and crashing and breaking, and the clock that never went now chiming on and on in horological frenzy. Above all, the joyous barking of chase and battle.

Andy held the door to, without clicking it shut, in case Teaser might want to get out in a hurry. But Teaser did not want to get out: he was in a terrier's paradise.

By now Andy's father and mother were out of bed again with Andy, and he explained what he had done. Mr. Potter was of the opinion that they should wait outside the room until Teaser had finished doing whatever he was doing. Mrs. Potter insisted that, in the meantime, Mr. Potter should fetch the poker from the sitting room. Then they waited until the barking and worrying noises grew less frequent. A kind of peace seemed to have come to the spare room.

Mr. Potter flung the door wide open, at the same time turning on the light.

The room was in a terrible mess: the bedspread had been torn off the bed, and the floor rugs were in a heap in one corner; the china rabbit and its litter were smashed and scattered all over the room; the cactus stood on its head in the middle of the floor, with earth and potsherds widely scattered around it; and the clock had been hurled from the mantelpiece and lay face-down on the floor in a mess of broken glass, still chiming. On the bed stood Teaser, panting, his mouth wide open with his tongue hanging out, his tail briskly wagging, his eyes shining. He was radiant, triumphant. The night of his life.

After a silence—"*They* won't come back," said Mr. Potter, "ever."

They tidied the bedroom as best they could. They repotted the cactus and threw away the remains of the rabbits and put the clock back on the mantelpiece. It would need a new glass, of course, but it had stopped chiming and was ticking quite sensibly. Mrs. Potter set it to the right time—almost breakfast time.

Later that day, visiting Aunt Enid in the hospital, Andy apologized for Teaser about the rabbits and the clock glass. He did not explain things. His mother had said that it would be best not to burden the invalid with the whole story.

Aunt Enid was not as prim as she used to be. She was naturally confused about what had been going on in the bungalow, but pleased. "I'm pleased that you and the dog had such a nice romp, Andy, dear," she said. "And when I'm home again, it'll be a great convenience that the clock really goes. I can easily get a new glass." She hesitated. "You had no trouble from—from *them*?"

Andy's father said quickly, "The dog got them."

# GABRIEL-ERNEST

## SAKI (H. H. MUNRO)

"THERE IS A wild beast in your woods," said the artist Cunningham as he was being driven to the station. It was the only remark that he had made during the drive, but as Van Cheele had talked incessantly, his companion's silence had not been noticeable.

"A stray fox or two and some resident weasels. Nothing more formidable," said Van Cheele. The artist said nothing.

"What did you mean about a wild beast?" said Van Cheele later, when they were on the platform.

"Nothing. My imagination. Here is the train," said Cunningham.

That afternoon Van Cheele went for one of his frequent rambles through his woodland property. He had a stuffed bittern in his study and knew the names of quite a number of wildflowers, so his aunt had possibly some justification in describing him as a great naturalist. At any rate, he was an avid walker. It was his custom to take mental notes of everything that he saw during his walks, not so much for the purpose of assisting contemporary science as to provide topics for conversation afterward. When the bluebells began to show themselves in flower, he made a point of informing everyone of the fact; the season of the year might have warned his hearers of the likelihood of such an occurrence, but at least they felt that he was being absolutely frank with them.

What Van Cheele saw on this particular afternoon was, however, something far removed from his ordinary range of experience. On a shelf of smooth stone overhanging a deep pool in the hollow of an oak coppice, a boy of around 16 lay sprawled, drying his wet brown limbs luxuriously in the sun. His wet hair, parted by a recent dive, lay close to his head, and his light brown eyes, so light that there was an almost tigerish gleam in them, were turned toward Van Cheele with a certain lazy watchfulness. It was an unexpected apparition, and Van Cheele found himself engaged in the novel process of thinking before he spoke. Where on earth could this wild-looking boy hail from? The miller's wife had lost a child some two months ago, supposed to have been swept away by the millrace, but that had been a mere baby, not a half-grown lad.

"What are you doing there?" he demanded.

"Obviously sunning myself," replied the boy.

"Where do you live?"

"Here, in these woods."

"You can't live in the woods," said Van Cheele.

"They are very nice woods," said the boy with a touch of patronage in his voice.

"But where do you sleep at night?"

"I don't sleep at night; that's my busiest time."

Van Cheele began to have an irritated feeling that he was grappling with a problem that was eluding him.

"What do you feed on?" he asked.

"Flesh," said the boy, and he pronounced the word with slow relish, as though he was tasting it.

"Flesh! What flesh?"

"Since it interests you, rabbits, wildfowl, hares, poultry, lambs in their season, children when I can get any; they're usually too well locked in at night, when I do most of my hunting. It's been two months since I tasted child flesh."

Ignoring the chaffing nature of the last remark, Van Cheele tried to draw the boy on the subject of possible poaching operations.

"You're talking rather through your hat when you speak of feeding on hares." (Considering the nature of the boy's toilet, the simile was hardly an apt one.) "Our hillside hares aren't easily caught."

"At night I hunt on four feet," was the somewhat cryptic response.

"I suppose you mean that you hunt with a dog?" hazarded Van Cheele.

The boy rolled slowly over onto his back and laughed a weird low laugh, which was pleasantly like a chuckle and disagreeably like a snarl.

"I don't think any dog would be very anxious for my company, especially at night."

Van Cheele began to feel that there was something positively uncanny about the strange-eyed, strange-tongued youngster.

"I can't have you staying in these woods," he declared authoritatively.

"I think you'd rather have me here than in your house," said the boy.

The prospect of this wild, nude animal in Van Cheele's primly ordered house was certainly an alarming one.

"If you don't go, I shall have to make you," said Van Cheele.

The boy turned like a flash, plunged into the pool, and in a moment had flung his wet and glistening body halfway up the bank where Van Cheele was standing. In an otter, the movement would not have been remarkable; in a boy, Van Cheele found it sufficiently startling. His foot slipped as he made an involuntary backward movement, and he found himself almost prostrate on the slippery weed-grown bank, with those tigerish yellow eyes not very far from his own. Almost instinctively, he half raised his hand to his throat. The boy laughed again, a laugh in which the snarl had almost driven out the chuckle and then, with another of his astonishing lightning movements, plunged out of view, into a yielding tangle of weeds and ferns.

"What an extraordinary wild animal!" said Van Cheele as he picked himself up. And then he recalled Cunningham's remark: "There is a wild beast in your woods."

Walking slowly homeward, Van Cheele began to turn over in his mind various local occurrences that might be traceable to the existence of this astonishing young savage.

Something had been thinning the game in the woods lately,

poultry had been missing from the farms, hares were growing unaccountably scarcer, and complaints had reached him of lambs being carried off bodily from the hills. Was it possible that this wild boy was really hunting the countryside in company with some clever poacher dog? He had spoken of hunting "four-footed" by night, but, then again, he had hinted strangely at no dog caring to come near him, "especially at night." It was certainly puzzling. And then, as Van Cheele ran his mind over the various depredations that had been committed during the last month or two, he came suddenly to a dead stop, alike in his walk and his speculations. The child missing from the mill two months ago—the accepted theory was that he had tumbled into the millrace and been swept away; but the mother had always declared that she had heard a shriek on the hillside of the house, in the opposite direction from the water. It was unthinkable, of course, but he wished that the boy had not made that uncanny remark about child flesh eaten two months ago. Such dreadful things should not be said even in fun.

Van Cheele, contrary to his usual wont, did not feel disposed to be communicative about his discovery in the wood. His position as a parish councilor and justice of the peace seemed somehow compromised by the fact that he was harboring a personality of such doubtful repute on his property; there was even a possibility that a heavy bill for damages for raided lambs and poultry might be laid at his door. At dinner that night he was quite unusually silent.

"Where's your voice gone to?" asked his aunt. "One would

think that you had seen a wolf."

Van Cheele, who was not familiar with the old saying, thought the remark rather foolish; if he *had* seen a wolf on his property, his tongue would have been extraordinarily busy with the subject.

At breakfast the next morning, Van Cheele was conscious that his feeling of uneasiness regarding yesterday's episode had not wholly disappeared, and he resolved to go by train to the neighboring cathedral town, hunt up Cunningham, and learn from him what he had really seen that had prompted the remark about a wild beast in the woods. With this resolution taken, his usual cheerfulness partially returned, and he hummed a bright little melody as he sauntered to the morning room for his customary cigarette. As he entered the room, the melody made way abruptly for a pious invocation. Gracefully sprawled on the ottoman, in an attitude of almost exaggerated repose, was the boy of the woods. He was drier than when Van Cheele had last seen him, but no other alteration was noticeable in him.

"How dare you come here?" asked Van Cheele furiously.

"You told me that I was not to stay in the woods," said the boy calmly.

"But not to come here. Supposing my aunt should see you!"

And with a view to minimizing that catastrophe, Van Cheele hastily obscured as much of his unwelcome guest as possible under the folds of a *Morning Post*. At that moment his aunt entered the room.

"This is a poor boy who has lost his way—and lost his

memory. He doesn't know who he is or where he comes from," explained Van Cheele desperately, glancing apprehensively at the waif's face to see whether he was going to add inconvenient candor to his other savage propensities.

Miss Van Cheele was enormously interested.

"Perhaps his underlinen is marked," she suggested.

"He seems to have lost most of that, too," said Van Cheele, making frantic little grabs at the *Morning Post* to keep it in its place.

A naked homeless child appealed to Miss Van Cheele as warmly as a stray kitten or derelict puppy would have done.

"We must do all we can for him," she decided, and in a very short time a messenger, dispatched to the rectory, where a pageboy was kept, had returned with a suit of pantry clothes and the necessary accessories of shirt, shoes, collar, etc. Clothed, clean, and groomed, the boy lost none of his uncanniness in Van Cheele's eyes, but his aunt found him sweet.

"We must call him something till we know who he really is," she said. "Gabriel-Ernest, I think; those are nice, suitable names."

Van Cheele agreed, but he privately doubted whether they were being grafted onto a nice, suitable child. His misgivings were not diminished by the fact that his staid and elderly spaniel had bolted out of the house at the first incoming of the boy and now obstinately remained shivering and yapping at the farther end of the orchard, while the canary, usually as vocally industrious as Van Cheele himself, had put itself on an allowance of frightened cheeps. More than ever he was resolved to consult

Cunningham without loss of time.

As he drove off to the station, his aunt was arranging that Gabriel-Ernest should help her entertain the infant members of her Sunday school class at tea that afternoon.

Cunningham was not at first disposed to be communicative.

"My mother died of some brain trouble," he explained, "so you will understand why I am averse to dwelling on anything of an impossibly fantastic nature that I may see or think that I have seen."

"But what did you see?" persisted Van Cheele.

"What I thought I saw was something so extraordinary that no really sane man could dignify it with the credit of it having actually happened. I was standing, the last evening I was with you, half hidden in the hedge growth by the orchard gate, watching the dying glow of the sunset. Suddenly I became aware of a naked boy, a bather from some neighboring pool, I took him to be, who was standing out on the bare hillside also watching the sunset. His pose was so suggestive of some wild faun of pagan myth that I instantly wanted to engage him as a model, and in another moment I think I should have hailed him. But just then the sun dipped out of view, and all of the orange and pink slid out of the landscape, leaving it cold and gray. And at the same moment an astounding thing happened—the boy vanished too!"

"What! Vanished away into nothing?" asked Van Cheele excitedly.

"No, that is the dreadful part of it," answered the artist; "on the open hillside, where the boy had been standing a second ago, stood a large wolf, blackish in color, with gleaming fangs and cruel, yellow eyes. You may think—"

But Van Cheele did not stop for anything as futile as thought. Already he was tearing at top speed toward the station. He dismissed the idea of a telegram. "Gabriel-Ernest is a werewolf" was a hopelessly inadequate effort at conveying the situation, and his aunt would think that it was a coded message to which he had omitted to give her the key. His one hope was that he might reach home before sundown. The cab that he chartered at the other end of the rail journey bore him with what seemed exasperating slowness along the country roads, which were pink and mauve with the flush of the sinking sun. His aunt was putting away some unfinished jams and cake when he arrived.

"Where is Gabriel-Ernest?" he almost screamed.

"He is taking the little Toop child home," said his aunt. "It was getting so late; I thought it wasn't safe to let him go back alone. What a lovely sunset, isn't it?"

But Van Cheele, although not oblivious to the glow in the western sky, did not stay to discuss its beauties. At a speed for which he was scarcely geared, he raced along the narrow lane that led to the home of the Toops. On one side ran the swift current of the millstream; on the other rose the stretch of bare hillside. A dwindling rim of red sun showed still on the skyline, and the next turning must bring him in view of the ill-assorted couple that he was pursuing. Then the color went suddenly out of things, and a gray light settled itself with a quick shiver over the landscape. Van

Cheele heard a shrill wail of fear and stopped running.

Nothing was ever seen again of the Toop child or Gabriel-Ernest, but the latter's discarded garments were found lying in the road, so it was assumed that the child had fallen into the water and that the boy had stripped and jumped in, in a vain endeavor to save him. Van Cheele and some workmen who were nearby at the time testified to having heard a child scream loudly just near the spot where the clothes were found. Mrs. Toop, who had 11 other children, was decently resigned to her bereavement, but Miss Van Cheele sincerely mourned her lost foundling. It was on her initiative that a memorial brass was put up in the parish church to "Gabriel-Ernest, an unknown boy who bravely sacrificed his life for another."

Van Cheele gave way to his aunt in most things, but he flatly refused to subscribe to the Gabriel-Ernest memorial.

# NULE

## JAN MARK

THE HOUSE WAS not old enough to be interesting, just old enough to be starting to fall apart. The few interesting things had been dealt with ages ago, when they first moved in. There was a bell push in every room, somehow connected to a glass case in the kitchen that contained a list of names and an indicator that wavered from name to name when a button was pushed, before settling on one of them: *Parlor; Drawing Room; Master Bedroom; Second Bedroom; Back Bedroom.*

"What are they for?" said Libby one morning, after roving around the house and pushing all of the buttons in turn. At that moment Martin pushed the button in the living room, and the indicator slid up to *Parlor,* vibrating there while the bell rang. And rang and rang.

"To fetch the maid," said Mum.

"We haven't got a maid."

"No, but you've got me," said Mum, and she tied an old sock over the bell so that afterward it would only whir instead of ring.

The mouse holes in the kitchen looked interesting too. The mice were bold and lounged around, making no effort at all to be timid and mouselike. They sat on the draining board in the evenings and could scarcely be bothered to stir themselves when the light was turned on.

"Easy living has made them soft," said Mum. "They have a gaming hall behind the boiler. They throw dice all day. They dance the cancan at night."

"Come off it," said Dad. "You'll be finding crates of tiny gin bottles next."

"They dance the cancan," Mum insisted. "Right over my head they dance it. I can hear them. If you didn't sleep so soundly, you'd hear them too."

"Oh, that. That's not mice," said Dad with a cheery smile. "That's rats."

Mum minded the mice less than the bells, until the day she found footprints in the frying pan.

"Sorry, boys, the party's over," she said to the mice, who were no doubt combing the dripping from their elegant whiskers at that very moment, and the mouse holes were blocked up.

Dad did the blocking up, and also some unblocking, so that after the bathtub no longer filled itself through the plug hole, the house stopped being interesting altogether, for a time.

Libby and Martin did what they could to improve matters. Beginning in the cupboard under the stairs, they worked their way through the house, up to the attic, looking for something; anything; tapping walls and floors, scouring cupboards, measuring and calculating, but there were no hidden cavities, no secret doors, no ambiguous bulges under the wallpaper, except where the dampness got in. The cupboard below the stairs was full of old pickle jars, and what they found in the attic didn't please anyone, least of all Dad.

"That's dry rot," he said. "Thank God this isn't our house," and he went cantering off to visit the real estate agents Tench and Tench. Dad called them Shark and Shark. As he got to the gate, he turned back and yelled, "The plague! The plague! Put a red cross on the door!" which made Mrs. Bowen, over the fence, lean right out of her landing window instead of hiding behind the curtains.

When Dad came back from the agents, he was growling.

"Shark junior says that since the whole row is coming down inside two years, it isn't worth bothering about. I understand that the new bypass is going to run right through the scullery."

"What did Shark senior say?" asked Mum.

"I didn't see him. I've never seen him. I don't believe that there is a Shark senior," said Dad. "I think he's dead. I think young Shark keeps him in a box under the bed."

"Don't be nasty," said Mum, looking at Libby, who worried about things under the bed even in broad daylight. "I just hope that we find a house of our own before this place collapses on our heads—and we won't be buying it from the Sharks."

She went back to her sewing, not in a good mood. The mice had broken out again. Libby went into the kitchen to look for them. Martin ran upstairs, rhyming:

> "*Mr. Shark,*
> *In the dark,*

*Under the bed.*
*Dead."*

When he came down again, Mum was putting away the sewing, and Libby was parading around the hall in a pointed hat with a veil and a long red dress that looked rich and splendid unless you knew, as Martin did, that it was made of old curtains.

The hall was dark in the rainy summer afternoon, and Libby slid from shadow to shadow, rustling.

"What are you supposed to be?" said Martin. "An old witch?"

"I'm Sleeping Beauty's mother," said Libby, and, lowering her head, she charged down the hall, pointed hat foremost, like a unicorn.

Martin changed his mind about walking downstairs and slid down the banister instead. He suspected that he would not be allowed to do this for much longer. Already the banister rail creaked, and who knew where the dreaded dry rot would strike next? As he reached the upright post at the bottom of the stairs, Mum came out of the back room, lugging the sewing machine, and just missed being impaled on Libby's hat.

"Stop rushing up and down," said Mum. "You'll ruin those clothes, and I've only just finished them. Go and take them off. And you," she said, turning to Martin, "stop swinging on that newel post. Do you want to tear it up by the roots?"

The newel post was supposed to be holding up the banister, but possibly it was the other way around. At the foot it was just a polished wooden post, but farther up it had been turned on a lathe, with slender hips, a waist, a bust almost, and square shoulders. On top was a round ball, as big as a head.

There was another one at the top of the stairs, but it had lost its head. Dad called it Anne Boleyn; the one at the bottom was simply a newel post, but Libby thought that this, too, was its name—Nule Post, like Anne Boleyn or Libby Anderson.

Mrs. Nule Post.

Lady Nule Post.

When she talked to it she just called it Nule.

The pointed hat and the old curtains were Libby's costume for the school play. Martin had managed to stay out of the school play, but he knew all of Libby's lines by heart as she chanted them around the house, up and down the stairs, in a strained, jerky voice, one syllable per step.

"My-dear-we-must-in-vite-all-the-fair-ies-to-the-christen-ing, hello, Nule, we-will-not-in-vite-the-wick-ed-fair-y!"

On the last day of the term, he sat with Mum and Dad in the school hall and watched Libby go through the same routine onstage. She was word-perfect, in spite of speaking as though her shock absorbers had collapsed, but as most of the cast spoke the same way, it didn't sound so very strange.

Once the school holidays began, Libby went back to talking like Libby, although she still wore the pointed hat and the curtains, until they began to fall to pieces. The curtains became dusters, but the pointed hat was around for a long time, until Mum picked it up and threatened, "Take this thing away, or it goes in the bin."

Libby shunted up and down the stairs a few times with the

hat on her head, and then Mum called out that Jane from next door had come to play. If Libby had been at the top of the stairs, she might have left the hat on her bed, but she was almost at the bottom, so she plonked it down on Nule's cannonball head and went out to fight Jane over whose turn it was to kidnap the teddy bear. She hoped that it was Jane's turn. If Libby was the kidnapper, she would have to sit around for ages holding Teddy to ransom behind the water tank, while Jane galloped around the garden on her imaginary pony, whacking the hydrangea bushes with a broomstick.

The hat definitely did something for Nule. When Martin came in later by the front door, he thought at first that it was a person standing at the foot of the stairs. He had to look twice before he understood who it was. Mum saw it at the same time.

"I told Libby to put that object away, or I'd throw it in the bin."

"Oh, don't," said Martin. "Leave it for Dad to see."

So she left it, but Martin began to get ideas. The hat made the rest of Nule look very undressed, so he fetched down the old housecoat that had been hanging behind the bathroom door when they moved in. It was purple, with blue paisleys swimming all over it, and very worn, as though it had been somebody's favorite housecoat. The sleeves had set-in creases around arms belonging to someone whom they had never known.

Turning it inside out, he buttoned it like a bib around Nule's neck so that it hung down to the floor. He filled two gloves with scrunched-up newspaper, poked them into the sleeves, and pinned them there. The weight made the arms dangle and opened the creases. He put a pair of soccer shoes under the hem of the housecoat, with the toes just sticking out, and stood back to see how it looked.

As he expected, in the darkness of the hall it looked just like a person, waiting, although there was something not so much lifelike as deathlike in the hang of those dangling arms.

Mum and Libby first saw Nule as they came out of the kitchen together.

"Who on earth did this?" said Mum as they drew alongside.

"It wasn't me," said Libby, and she sounded very glad that it wasn't.

"It was you who left the hat, wasn't it?"

"Yes, but not the other things."

"What do you think?" said Martin.

"Horrible thing," said Mum, but she didn't ask him to take it down. Libby sidled around Nule and ran upstairs, as close to the wall as she could get.

When Dad came home from work, he stopped in the doorway and said, "Hello—who's that? Who . . . ?" before Martin turned on the light and showed him.

"An idol, I suppose," said Dad. "Nule, god of dry rot," and he bowed low at the foot of the stairs. At the same time the hat slipped forward slightly, as if Nule had lowered its head in acknowledgment. Martin also bowed low before reaching up to set the hat straight.

Mum and Dad seemed to think that Nule was rather funny, so it stayed at the foot of the stairs. They never bowed to it again, but Martin did, every time he went upstairs, and so did Libby. Libby didn't talk to Nule anymore, but she watched it a lot. One day she said, "Which way is it facing?"

"Forward, of course," said Martin, but it was hard to tell unless you looked at the feet. He drew two staring eyes and a toothy smile on a piece of paper and cut them out. They were attached to the front of Nule's head with little pieces of chewing gum.

"*That's* better," said Libby, laughing, and the next time she went upstairs, she forgot to bow. Martin was not so sure. Nule looked ordinary now, just like a newel post wearing a housecoat, soccer shoes, and Sleeping Beauty's mother's hat. He took off the eyes and the mouth and rubbed away the chewing gum.

"That's better," he said, while Nule stared once more without eyes and smiled without a mouth.

Libby said nothing.

At night the house creaked.

"Thiefly footsteps," said Libby.

"It's the furniture warping," said Mum.

Libby thought she said that the furniture was walking, and she could well believe it. The dressing table had feet with claws; why shouldn't it walk in the dark, tugging fretfully this way and that, because the clawed feet pointed in opposite directions? The bathtub had feet too. Libby imagined it galloping out of the bathroom and tobogganing downstairs on its stomach, like a great white walrus plunging into the sea. If someone held the door open, it would whiz up the path and crash into the front gate. If someone held the gate open, it would shoot across the road and hit the neighbor's car, which she parked under the streetlight opposite.

Libby thought of headlines in the local paper—NURSE RUN OVER BY BATHTUB—and giggled, until she heard the creaks again. Then she hid under the covers.

In his bedroom Martin heard the creaks too, but he had a different reason for worrying. In the attic where the dry rot lurked, there was a big oak wardrobe full of old dead ladies' clothes. It was directly over his head. Supposing it came through?

The next day he moved the bed.

The vacuum cleaner had lost its wheels and had to be helped, by Libby pushing from behind. It skidded up the hall and knocked Nule's soccer shoes askew.

"The vacuum doesn't like Nule either," said Libby. Although she wouldn't talk to Nule anymore, she liked talking *about* it, as though that somehow made Nule safer.

"What's that?" said Mum.

"It knocked Nule's feet off."

"Well, put them back," said Mum, but Libby preferred not to. When Martin came in, he set them side by side, but later they were kicked out of place again. If people began to complain that Nule was in the way, Nule would have to go. He got around this by putting the right shoe where the left had been and the left shoe on the bottom stair. When he left it, the veil on the hat was hanging down behind, but as he went upstairs after dinner, he noticed that it was now draped over Nule's right shoulder, as if Nule had turned its head to see where its feet were going.

That night the creaks were louder than ever, like a burglar on hefty tiptoe. Libby had mentioned thieves only that evening, and Mum had said, "What do we have worth stealing?"

Martin felt fairly safe because he had figured out that if the wardrobe fell tonight, it would land on his chest of drawers and not on him, but what might it bring down with it? Then he realized that the creaks were coming not from above but from below.

He held his breath. Downstairs didn't creak.

His alarm clock gleamed greenly in the dark and told him that it had passed two o'clock. Mum and Dad were asleep ages ago. Libby would sooner burst than leave her bed in the dark. Perhaps it *was* a burglar. Feeling noble and reckless, he turned on the bedside lamp, slid out of bed, and walked silently across the carpet. He turned on the main light and opened the door. The glow shone out of the doorway and saw him as far as the landing light switch at the top of the stairs, but he never had time to turn it on. From the top of the stairs he could look down into the hall where the streetlight opposite shone coldly through the frosted panes of the front door.

It shone on the hall stand where the coats hung, on the

blanket chest, and on the brass jug that stood on it, through the white coins of the honesty plants in the brass jug, and on the broody telephone that never rang at night. It did not shine on Nule. Nule was not there.

Nule was halfway up the stairs, one hand on the banisters and one hand holding up the housecoat, clear of its shoes. The veil on the hat drifted like smoke across the frosted glass of the front door. Nule creaked and came up another step.

Martin turned and fled back to the bedroom and dived under the covers, just like Libby, who was three years younger and believed in ghosts.

"Were you reading in bed last night?" said Mum, prodding him awake the next morning. Martin came out from under the pillow, very slowly.

"No, Mum."

"You went to sleep with the light on. *Both* lights," she said, leaning across to turn off the one by the bed.

"I'm sorry."

"Perhaps you'd like to pay the next electricity bill?"

Mum had brought him a cup of tea, which meant that she had been down to the kitchen and back again, unscathed. Martin wanted to ask her if there was anything strange on the stairs, but he didn't quite know how to put it. He drank the tea, got dressed, and went along the landing.

He looked down into the hall where the sun shone through the frosted glass of the front door, on to the hall stand, the blanket chest, the honesty plants in the brass jug, and the telephone that began to ring as he looked at it. It shone on Nule, standing with its back to him at the foot of the stairs.

Mum came out of the kitchen to answer the phone, and Martin went down and stood three steps up, watching Nule and waiting for Mum to finish talking. Nule looked just as it always did. Both feet were back on ground level, side by side.

"I wish you wouldn't hang around like that when I'm on the phone," said Mum, putting down the receiver and turning around. "Eavesdropper. Breakfast will be ready in five minutes."

She went back into the kitchen, and Martin sat on the blanket chest, looking at Nule. It was time for Nule to go. He should walk up to Nule this minute, kick away the shoes, rip off the housecoat, throw away the hat, but . . .

He stayed where he was, watching the motionless soccer shoes, the dangling sleeves. The breeze from an open window stirred the hem of the housecoat and revealed the wooden post beneath, rooted firmly in the floor as it had been for 70 years.

There were no feet in the shoes, no arms in the sleeves.

If he destroyed Nule, it would mean that he believed that he had seen Nule climbing the stairs last night, but if he left Nule alone, Nule might walk again.

He had a problem.

# THE DANCING PARTNER

JEROME K. JEROME

"THIS STORY," COMMENCED MacShaugnassy, "comes from Furtwangen, a small town in the Black Forest.

"There lived there a very wonderful old fellow named Nicholau Geibel. His business was the making of mechanical toys, at which work he had acquired an almost European reputation. He made rabbits that would emerge from the heart of a cabbage, flop their ears, smooth their whiskers, and disappear again; cats that would wash their faces and meow so naturally that dogs would mistake them for real cats and fly at them; dolls, with phonographs concealed within them, that would raise their hats and say, 'Good morning; how do you do?' and some that would even sing a song.

"But he was something more than a mere mechanic; he was an artist. His work was for him a hobby, almost a passion. His shop was filled with all manner of strange things that never would, or could, be sold—things that he had made for the pure love of making them. He had contrived a mechanical donkey that would trot for two hours by means of stored electricity and trot too much faster than the live article and with less need for exertion on the part of the driver; a bird that would shoot up into the air, fly around and around in a circle, and drop to the earth at the exact spot from where it started; a skeleton that, supported by an upright iron bar, would dance a hornpipe; a life-size lady doll that could play the fiddle; and a gentleman with a hollow inside who could smoke a pipe and drink more beer than any three average German students put together, which is saying much.

"Indeed, it was the belief of the town that old Geibel could make a man capable of doing everything that a respectable man need want to do. One day he made a man who did too much, and it came about in this way:

"Young Doctor Follen had a baby, and the baby had a birthday. His first birthday put Doctor Follen's household into somewhat of a flurry, but on the occasion of his second birthday, Mrs. Doctor Follen gave a ball in honor of the event. Old Geibel and his daughter, Olga, were among the guests.

"During the afternoon of the next day some three or four of Olga's bosom friends, who had also been present at the ball, dropped in to have a chat about it. They naturally fell to discussing the men and to criticizing their dancing. Old Geibel was in the room, but he appeared to be absorbed in his newspaper, and the girls took no notice of him.

" 'There seems to be fewer men who can dance at every ball you go to,' said one of the girls.

" 'Yes, and don't the ones who can give themselves airs?' said another. 'They make quite a favor of asking you.'

" 'And how stupidly they talk,' added a third. 'They always say exactly the same things: "How charming you are looking tonight." "Do you often go to Vienna? Oh, you should, it's delightful." "What a charming dress you have on." "What a warm day it has been." "Do you like Wagner?" I do wish they'd think of something new.'

" 'Oh, I never mind how they talk,' said a fourth. 'If a man dances well, he may be a fool for all I care.'

" 'He generally is,' slipped in a thin girl, rather spitefully.

" 'I go to a ball to dance,' continued the previous speaker, not noticing the interruption. 'All I ask of a partner is that he shall hold me firmly, take me around steadily, and not get tired before I do.'

" 'A clockwork figure would be the thing for you,' said the girl who had interrupted.

" 'Bravo!' cried one of the others, clapping her hands. 'What a capital idea!'

" 'What's a capital idea?' they asked.

" 'Why, a clockwork dancer or, better yet, one that would go by electricity and never run down.'

"The girls took up the idea with enthusiasm.

" 'Oh, what a lovely partner he would make,' said one; 'he would never kick you or step on your toes.'

" 'Or tear your dress,' said another.

" 'Or get out of step.'

" 'Or get giddy and lean on you.'

" 'And he would never want to mop his face with his handkerchief. I do hate to see a man do that after every dance.'

"'And wouldn't want to spend the whole evening in the supper room.'

"'Why, with a phonograph inside him to grind out all of the stock remarks, you would not be able to tell him from a real man,' said the girl who had first suggested the idea.

"'Oh, yes, you would,' said the thin girl; 'he would be so much nicer.'

"Old Geibel had laid down his paper and was listening with both of his ears. Upon one of the girls glancing in his direction, however, he hurriedly hid himself again behind it.

"After the girls were gone, he went into his workshop, where Olga heard him walking up and down and every now and then chuckling to himself; and that night he talked to her a good deal about dancing and dancing men—asked what they usually said and did—what dances were most the popular—what steps were gone through, with many other questions bearing on the subject.

"Then for a couple of weeks he kept much to his factory and was very thoughtful and busy, though prone at unexpected moments to break into a quiet, low laugh, as if enjoying a joke that nobody else knew of.

"A month later another ball took place in Furtwangen. On this occasion it was given by old Wenzel, the wealthy timber merchant, to celebrate his niece's betrothal, and Geibel and his daughter were again among the invited.

"When the hour arrived to set out, Olga sought her father. Not finding him in the house, she tapped on the door of his workshop. He appeared in his shirtsleeves, looking hot but radiant.

" 'Don't wait for me,' he said. 'You go on. I'll follow you; I've got something to finish.'

"As she turned to obey, he called after her, 'Tell them I'm going to bring a young man with me—such a nice young man, and an excellent dancer. All of the girls will like him.' Then he laughed and closed the door.

"Her father generally kept his doings secret from everybody, but she had a pretty shrewd suspicion of what he had been planning and so, to a certain extent, was able to prepare the guests for what was coming. Anticipation ran high, and the arrival of the famous mechanist was eagerly awaited.

"At length the sound of wheels was heard outside, followed by a great commotion in the passage, and old Wenzel himself, his jolly face red with excitement and suppressed laughter, burst into the room and announced in stentorian tones, 'Herr Geibel— and a friend.'

"Herr Geibel and his 'friend' entered, greeted with shouts of laughter and applause, and advanced to the center of the room.

" 'Allow me, ladies and gentlemen,' said Herr Geibel, 'to introduce you to my friend, Lieutenant Fritz. Fritz, my dear fellow, bow to the ladies and gentlemen.'

"Geibel placed his hand encouragingly on Fritz's shoulder, and the lieutenant bowed low, accompanying the action with a harsh clicking noise in his throat, unpleasantly suggestive of a death rattle. But that was only a detail.

" 'He walks a little stiffly' (Old Geibel took his arm and

walked him forward a few steps; he certainly did walk stiffly), 'but, then walking, is not his forte. He is essentially a dancing man. I have only been able to teach him the waltz as yet, but at that he is faultless. Come, which of you ladies may I introduce him to as a partner? He keeps perfect time; he never gets tired; he won't kick you or step on your dress; he will hold you as firmly as you like and go as quickly or as slowly as you please; he never gets giddy; and he is full of conversation. Come, speak up for yourself, my boy.'

"The old gentleman twisted one of the buttons at the back of his coat, and immediately Fritz opened his mouth and, in thin tones that appeared to proceed from the back of his head, remarked suddenly, 'May I have the pleasure?' and then shut his mouth again with a snap.

"That Lieutenant Fritz had made a strong impression on the company was undoubted, yet none of the girls seemed inclined to dance with him. They looked askance at his waxen face, with its staring eyes and fixed smile, and shuddered. At last old Geibel came to the girl who had conceived the idea.

"'It is your own suggestion, carried out to the letter,' said Geibel. 'An electric dancer. You owe it to the gentleman to give him a trial.'

"She was a bright, saucy little girl, fond of a frolic. Her host added his entreaties, and she consented.

"Herr Geibel fixed the figure to her. Its right arm was screwed around her waist and held her firmly; its delicately joined left hand was made to fasten itself upon her right. The old toy maker showed her how to regulate its speed and how to stop it and release her.

" 'It will take you around in a complete circle,' he explained, 'but be careful that no one knocks against you and alters its course.'

"The music struck up. Old Geibel put the current in motion, and Annette and her strange partner began to dance.

"For a while everyone stood watching them. The figure performed its purpose admirably. Keeping perfect time and step and holding its little partner tight, clasped in an unyielding embrace, it revolved steadily, pouring forth at the same time a constant flow of squeaky conversation, broken by brief intervals of grinding silence.

" 'How charming you are looking tonight,' it remarked in its thin, faraway voice. 'What a lovely day it has been. Do you like dancing? How well our steps agree. You will give me another, won't you? Oh, don't be so cruel. What a charming gown you have on. Isn't waltzing delightful? I could go on dancing forever—with you. Have you had supper?'

"As she grew more familiar with the uncanny creature, the girl's nervousness wore off, and she entered into the fun of the thing.

" 'Oh, he's just lovely,' she cried, laughing. 'I could go on dancing with him all my life.'

"Couple after couple now joined them, and soon all of the dancers in the room were whirling around behind them. Nicholau Geibel stood looking on, beaming with childish delight at his success.

"Old Wenzel approached him and whispered something in his ear, Geibel laughed and nodded, and the two worked their way quietly toward the door.

"'This is the young people's house tonight,' said Wenzel as soon as they were outside; 'you and I will have a quiet pipe and a glass of wine, over at the countinghouse.'

"Meanwhile, the dancing grew more fast and furious. Little Annette loosened the screw regulating her partner's rate of progress, and the figure flew around with her, swifter and swifter. Couple after couple dropped out exhausted, but they only went the faster, till at length they remained dancing alone.

"Madder and madder became the waltz. The music lagged behind: the musicians, unable to keep pace, ceased and sat staring. The younger guests applauded, but the older faces began to grow anxious.

"'Hadn't you better stop, dear?' said one of the women. 'You'll make yourself so tired.'

"But Annette did not answer.

"'I believe she's fainted,' cried out a girl who had caught sight of her face as it was swept by.

"One of the men sprang forward and clutched at the figure, but its impetus threw him down onto the floor, where its steel-cased feet laid bare his cheek. The thing evidently did not intend to part with its prize easily.

"Had anyone retained a cool head, the figure, one cannot help thinking, might easily have been stopped. Two or three men acting in concert might have lifted it bodily off the floor or jabbed it into a corner. But few human heads are capable of remaining cool under excitement. Those who are not present think how stupid must have been those who were; those who are reflect afterward how simple it would have been to do this, that, or the other, if only they had thought of it at the time.

"The women grew hysterical. The men shouted contradictory directions to one another. Two of them made a bungling rush at the figure, which had the result of forcing it out of its orbit in the center of the room and sending it crashing against the walls and furniture. A stream of blood showed itself down the girl's white frock and followed her along the floor. The affair was becoming horrible. The women rushed screaming from the room. The men followed them.

"One sensible suggestion was made: 'Find Geibel—fetch Geibel.'

"No one had noticed him leave the room; no one knew where he was. A party went in search of him. The others, too unnerved to go back into the ballroom, crowded outside the door and listened. They could hear the steady whir of the wheels upon the polished floor as the thing spun around and around; the dull thud as every now and again it dashed itself and its burden against some opposing object and ricocheted off in a new direction.

"And everlastingly it talked in that thin, ghostly voice, repeating over and over the same formula: 'How charming you are looking tonight. What a lovely day it has been. Oh, don't be so cruel. I could go on dancing forever—with you. Have you had supper?'

"Of course they looked for Geibel everywhere but where he was. They looked in every room in the house, and then they rushed off in a body to his own place and spent precious minutes in waking up his deaf old housekeeper. At last it occurred to one of the party that Wenzel was missing also, and then the idea of the countinghouse across the yard presented itself to them, and there they found him.

"He rose up, very pale, and followed them; and he and old Wenzel forced their way through the crowd of guests gathered outside, and entered the room, and locked the door behind them.

"From within there came the muffled sound of low voices and quick steps, followed by a confused scuffling noise, then silence, then the low voices again.

"After a time the door opened, and those near it pressed forward to enter, but old Wenzel's broad shoulders barred the way.

" 'I want you—and you, Bekler,' he said, addressing a couple of the older men. His voice was calm, but his face was deadly white. 'The rest of you, please go—get the women away as quickly as you can.'

"From that day old Nicholau Geibel confined himself to the making of mechanical rabbits and cats that meowed and washed their faces."

# THE RING

## MARGARET BINGLEY

THE MOMENT THAT Kate set eyes on the ring she knew that she had to have it. She wasn't normally interested in old-fashioned jewelry, but this was different. It was a small gold band with a ruby-red stone set in the center, surrounded by tiny diamondlike chips, and its timeless elegance appealed to the Kate that she longed to be. That Kate was tall and slender, not short and slightly plump; she was witty and popular at dances and parties, instead of quiet and always on the fringe of things. This ring seemed to symbolize everything she hoped that she would one day become, and she had the ridiculous feeling that if she could own it—actually wear it on her finger—then all of these things would be possible.

The jewelry shop itself was new. It had opened only a month ago, and although Kate and her friends passed it every day on their way home from school, they'd never really studied the window display before. Kate had left school early that day for a dental appointment and was dawdling along killing time, so she'd stopped to look in the window, and once she had looked, she was lost.

Her 16th birthday was in two weeks' time, and so far she hadn't been able to decide what she wanted as a present from her mother and Steve. Steve was her stepfather, and Kate liked him, but she was still close to her dad. He'd remarried too, straight after the divorce six years earlier, and he and his second wife, Lizzie, lived a few streets away with their four-year-old twin sons, Jake and Ben. They'd give her money for her birthday—they always did. Kate's mum, Louise, said that it was because they were too busy with the twins to find time to choose a present, but she and Steve always gave Kate presents, and so possession of the ring was a real possibility.

Before she mentioned it at home, she took her two best friends, Samantha and Clare, to look at the ring. They didn't seem as impressed as she was.

"It's a bit old-fashioned," said Samantha. "They've got better rings at the jewelry stall in the market on Saturdays. Really shiny ones, and much bigger than that."

Kate, normally a very placid girl, felt an unaccustomed rush of anger. "I don't want cheap stuff. I want a nice ring!" she snapped.

Samantha and Clare glanced at each other in surprise, and Clare decided not to say that she thought it was hideous and more like something her grandmother would wear. "It's certainly different, Kate," she said tactfully, "but I bet it's dreadfully expensive. Antique jewelry always is."

Kate hadn't thought of that, and her stomach did a kind of dip, as though she was on a roller-coaster ride at the fair. "How expensive?" she asked.

Clare shrugged. "I don't know; probably a couple of hundred pounds. Isn't there a price tag on it?" The three girls peered into the window, but nothing on display was priced.

"That's sure to mean it costs a fortune," said Samantha. "It's like that posh dress shop on the high street. They don't show prices either, but Mum says they charge you just for walking inside!" Both she and Clare laughed. Kate didn't. To her friends' astonishment, she was opening the shop door and marching inside, leaving them alone in the street.

"She's in a funny mood," said Samantha.

Clare sighed. "Probably because she hasn't got a boyfriend." Then they smiled at each other, confident that they looked good and that boys were attracted to them. "She'd be okay if she'd dress better and chat more," continued Clare, "but she doesn't seem to try."

"She's fed up because Jeff hasn't asked her out yet," muttered Samantha. "If only she'd come out of her shell a bit, she'd do much better. There's nothing really wrong with her."

"No, but then there's nothing really right either!" exclaimed Clare, and Kate's two supposed friends collapsed in giggles in the street outside the shop.

Inside the shop, totally unaware of her friends' derision, Kate was standing in front of the glass-topped counter, her heart thumping erratically as she faced the most handsome man she'd ever seen. She'd expected the owner to be a small, wizened old man with glasses, not a tall, dark man in his early 30s whose brown eyes skimmed over her with seeming admiration, while his lips parted in a warm smile.

"How can I help you, young lady?" he asked gently. His voice was deep and rich, like an actor's.

Kate swallowed hard. Her friends were right, she thought; everything inside the shop spoke of money. She must have been stupid to imagine that her mum and Steve could afford to buy anything that was on sale here, and if she hadn't been transfixed by the magnetism of the owner's gaze, she would have turned and run.

"It's the ring!" she blurted out.

His eyes widened a fraction; the dark pupils seemed to expand as he stared at her with even more interest so that a small tingle ran through her. "Which ring would that be?" he asked softly. "I do have quite a few."

Kate knew that this was true, yet she had the totally illogical feeling that he knew which ring she meant and knew that it was meant for her just as certainly as she knew it. "The old one with the red stone in the middle. It's in the left-hand corner of the window," she said in a rush.

He nodded. "Ah, yes, *that* ring. It is very attractive and has quite a history, too. Many, many people have worn that ring."

"How do you know?" asked Kate.

He gave a short laugh. "Because it's old, of course!"

"I suppose that means it's very expensive," said Kate despondently.

"Well, now, that depends on what you call expensive. In terms of money, I would say it was quite cheap."

Kate frowned. She didn't understand how it could be expensive in any other way besides money. Expensive things cost a lot. As far as she knew, there wasn't any other way in which the ring could be expensive, but then Kate was not yet 16, and she still had a lot to learn.

"How much is it?" she asked bravely, bracing herself for disappointment.

"I take it it's for you?" queried the owner.

"Oh, yes! You see, it's my sixteenth birthday soon, and this would be the most perfect present, only we don't have . . . well, my parents are divorced and all that. I mean, we aren't poor or anything, but I've got stepsisters at home now and twin half brothers at my dad's, and so the money has to stretch further and . . ." She stopped, appalled at what she'd said. How could she start telling a perfect stranger all of these things about her family, things that she never discussed with anyone, not even Samantha and Clare?

The man nodded. "It happens a lot these days. I tell you what, you try it on for size, and if it fits, if there's no need for any alteration, then you can tell your mother that it's . . ." He stopped and stared at her for a moment. "How about twenty pounds?" he suggested.

Kate shivered with a mixture of excitement and fear. Twenty pounds was exactly what Steve had told her that they could afford to spend. She'd felt a bit put out because Laura, his 12-year-old daughter from his first marriage, had gotten a computer for her birthday, and that had certainly cost more than 20 pounds, but then she'd pushed the thought away because Steve always treated her like his own daughter in other ways.

"Twenty pounds would be perfect," she said to the man.

He turned toward the window and brought the ring up to the counter. Close up, it looked even better. Although Kate knew that it couldn't be real gold for that price, the band had a warm glow about it, and the red stone in the middle was dark, while the small pieces of glass around it glittered with reflected light.

"Which finger did you want to wear it on?" he asked her.

Without thinking, Kate held out the ring finger of her right hand. He took the ring from its box and slid it carefully over the nail. Kate held her breath in painful excitement. It looked much too small to fit her finger, and she wished that she'd said the little finger, where it might have stood more of a chance. She felt her hand begin to tremble in the man's, and his unusually long fingers tightened, holding her hand steady as the ring continued its progress. It seemed to the startled Kate that the ring actually changed shape as he moved it, expanding to fit her and gliding smoothly over the knuckle until it came to rest just beneath the joint.

She stared down at it, and her whole hand felt warm. Somehow the ring seemed to change the look of her hand in the way that she'd hoped. It seemed slimmer and more elegant, less the slightly pudgy hand of an adolescent and more like that of a rich lady of leisure.

"A perfect fit!"

Kate could hear the satisfaction in the man's voice, and she smiled at him. "It's gorgeous. I think it looks even better on than off. Will you keep it for me until Mum can come in and pay for it?" she added anxiously.

"Of course. The ring is most definitely yours."

"I'd better take it off," said Kate, but it fit more snugly than she'd expected and proved difficult to move.

"Allow me," said the shop owner, and once again his long fingers closed around her hand, and another tingle ran through her as he slid it off easily and put it back inside its box.

"You'd better take my name," said Kate breathlessly. He nodded, writing down her details as she gave them to him, but she had the weird feeling that he already knew everything there was to know about her.

As he placed the ring back inside its box, now labeled with her name, she had one small moment of unease, a premonition that perhaps this had all gone too easily. Somehow the price seemed too low and the fit too perfect, but she brushed the thought away. How could anything be too good?

"I'll tell my mum tonight," she promised the man. "She should be able to get here tomorrow or Saturday, at the latest."

He nodded, obviously quite confident that the ring would be collected and paid for. At the doorway, Kate stopped for a moment. "Why is it so cheap?" she asked hesitantly. "I mean, even colored glass costs money, and it's so well made. Everything looks real."

The man nodded. "Lots of things that seem real aren't; people, too, I find. Besides, I never said that it was a cheap ring!" He laughed softly, more to himself than to Kate.

"It is really old, though, isn't it?" persisted Kate, wondering why on earth she was doing this when she wanted it so much. It was just that there was definitely something making her uneasy.

He looked steadily at her. "Very old," he confirmed. "Perhaps you'd be happier if I charged you more?" he added.

"No!" exclaimed Kate. "No, honestly. I suppose I can't believe my luck."

"I hope you enjoy your birthday," he said evenly, and as the door closed behind her, he smiled to himself before putting the boxed ring carefully inside his safe. He considered that he'd just made a very good sale.

Outside the shop, Samantha and Clare were far from happy. "You took ages!" complained Clare as they hurried home. "What on earth were you doing?"

"I tried it on, and it fit," said Kate happily.

"How much?" asked Samantha sourly.

"Only twenty pounds, so that's all right. It means I can have it!"

Her friends had never seen her so elated. Neither of them would have been seen dead wearing the ring, but they didn't say as much to Kate. It would only cause trouble, and at least she'd get a decent present this year. Last year she'd gotten a hair dryer, which they'd all agreed was pretty mean, even if it did free the other one for the rest of the family. Hair dryers were boring, everyday necessities. Rings, even weird ones, were proper presents.

As Kate had anticipated, her mother and Steve were delighted to hear that she'd found a present she wanted, and the very next day her mother went off and collected the ring. When she got home, Louise told Steve that it was very pretty, but not at all what she'd have expected Kate to choose.

"I'm sure it's valuable, too," she added when he'd buried himself in the sports pages of the newspaper. "For one thing, it's hallmarked, and the stone in the middle looks remarkably like a real ruby."

"Perhaps the guy doesn't know what he's doing," said Steve, without much interest. "The main thing is, we got it for twenty pounds, and Kate will be happy."

"I suppose so. It's only . . . " Louise's voice trailed away when she realized that Steve still wasn't listening. She couldn't blame him. Why look a gift horse in the mouth? And they were lucky that Kate was such an easygoing girl, never resenting the fact that Steve's two daughters had more spent on them or that her father's second wife didn't ever seem that pleased to have her stay for more than a day at a time.

Sometimes Louise felt really sorry for Kate, but at other times her daughter's lack of self-confidence irritated her. Steve's girls were so different. They were both lively and quick, did well at school, and were popular. They were easy to be proud of, but they weren't her children, and Kate was her own flesh and blood. She knew that the divorce hadn't helped, but sometimes she found herself wishing that Kate was less like her father, both physically and mentally. Not that she'd ever let her daughter know how she felt. It was one of those secret things that she kept firmly locked away most of the time, and she knew that Kate had absolutely no idea that she disappointed her mother.

On the morning of her birthday, Kate was awake early, and for the first time in several years she felt fizzy with excitement. Today she'd actually get the ring, and as it was a Saturday, she could wear it all weekend. She was hoping to wear it at school as well, but if they had a routine clampdown on jewelry, she'd have to leave it off for a while. It never crossed her mind that this might not be possible.

At eight o'clock all of the family piled into her bedroom, her mother carrying a tray with cups of tea and treats, the usual birthday-morning routine.

"Happy birthday, darling!" she said with a wide smile.

"Happy birthday, Kate!" shouted Sara, Steve's ten-year-old daughter, while Laura kissed her on the cheek and said, "You're getting really old now, Katie!" which made them all laugh. Lots of presents and cards were put on her bed, but Kate simply couldn't wait any longer and fell on the tiny, beautifully wrapped box that her mother had put beside her. She tore desperately at the glossy paper and ripped off the gold bow, like a starving person falling on food.

"Steady there!" said Steve, made slightly nervous by the feverish way that his stepdaughter was scrabbling at the present, but when she lifted the lid of the box, he saw the ring and whistled softly to himself. No wonder Louise had been surprised at the price. It did look really valuable, a genuine antique.

Even Sara and Laura were silenced by the ring's beauty and watched breathlessly as Kate slipped it over her finger. For Kate, this was one of the best moments of her life. She couldn't remember when she'd last wanted something so much, and she stretched out her hand, noticing once again how much slimmer it looked with the ring in place.

"It's beautiful, darling!" said her mother. Kate lifted her head for a kiss, and as her mother's smiling face moved toward her, she quite clearly heard her say, *What a pity her fingers are so fat.*

Kate gasped. Her mother's lips hadn't moved, she was still smiling and moving toward her, and yet the words had been said. Kate drew back, tears prickling in her eyes.

"Darling, whatever's wrong? It looks lovely, doesn't it, Steve?"

"Fantastic!" agreed Steve heartily. "Come on, Kate, give me a birthday kiss." Bewildered, Kate turned toward Steve. He had his arms outstretched, and he, too, was smiling, but even as he smiled, she heard him say, *And unless I'm very much mistaken, I'm the only man apart from her father who'll kiss her today. She really ought to do something to smarten herself up.*

Kate's throat seemed to be closing, and there was a hammering at her temples. She gave a tiny cry and drew back from both Steve and her mother. They glanced at each other in consternation, but Sara and Laura, totally unaware that anything was wrong, pushed their present into Kate's hands.

"Here you are, Katie. We hope you like it," said Sara.

With hands that were shaking, but from shock now instead of excitement, Kate unwrapped their present. It was a tube of liquid foundation, one of a new range that she'd been thinking about trying. Her mother was always saying that young girls didn't need much makeup, but Kate knew that the girls who did the best at parties were the ones who were heavily made up. You couldn't be sophisticated with the freshly scrubbed look of a ten year old.

"Do you like it?" asked Laura, jumping up and down.

"It's great. Thanks."

Sara began to examine the ring on Kate's hand. *We thought it might help cover your zits!* she said with a snicker.

Kate pulled back her hand sharply. "I don't get zits!" she protested.

They all looked at her in surprise. "No one said you did, Kate," said her mother gently.

"Sara did!"

Sara looked frightened and backed away from Kate's bed. "I didn't! I didn't say anything!"

"Mum?" Kate's voice was high with fright.

Sara continued to stare at her stepsister in astonishment, and even as Kate's mother reassured her that no one had mentioned zits, Sara's voice rang through Kate's head as clear as a bell.

*She heard what I was thinking!*

Kate's head whipped around, and she looked at Sara in amazement. Suddenly her head was full of voices. Her mother's sounded irritated as she muttered, *What on earth's the matter with her now? Why can't she be happy for once?* while Steve's was lighter, although the words were desperately hurtful: *Thank God she's not my own daughter!* In the background she could hear both of her stepsisters wishing that she'd hurry up and go to her father's for the rest of the day, and in a sudden moment of blinding clarity, Kate realized what was happening.

It was the ring.

She tried to remember what the man in the shop had said. Something about nothing in life being what it seemed, not even people. Kate was beginning to understand what he'd meant by that.

She was about to tear the ring off her finger when the voices subsided. Everyone was still looking at her oddly, and there was a strained atmosphere in the bedroom, but thankfully the voices had stopped.

"Are you all right, Kate?" asked her mother anxiously.

Kate nodded. There wasn't anything that she could say to them to explain her behavior, and perhaps it wasn't the ring. Maybe she'd gotten overexcited about the present and imagined it all or at the very worst picked up some of their thoughts by accident, like a mistuned radio or something. It couldn't really be the ring; that was ridiculous. In fact, now that everything was normal again, she decided that nothing had happened. She'd imagined it all. She must have, otherwise how could she continue living in a house where the people who were supposed to love her best said one thing and thought another?

Kate shook her head. "I'm sorry; I don't know what

happened. I felt really odd, but I'm fine now. Must have been too much excitement."

"Do you still want to go to your dad's?" asked Louise. "Would you rather spend the day with us?"

Inside Kate's head she heard someone groan. "No, honestly, I'm fine," she said quickly. "Besides, Lizzie's cooking a special lunch. I can't let them down."

"She wants to get her hands on her birthday money!" joked Steve, breaking the tension in the room. Everyone laughed. After that, Kate opened the remaining presents, looked through her cards, and, when the others had gone, pulled on her bathrobe and went into the bathroom to take a shower.

It was then that she discovered that the ring wouldn't come off.

It had gone on easily enough, but now it was gripping her finger like a vise, and the harder she tugged, the tighter it seemed to get. She put some soap around the edge and tried to ease it over the joint, but that didn't work. In the end, with Sara hammering on the door saying that she wanted to use the bathroom, she had to give up and shower with it on. She was terrified that it would get spoiled, but when she stepped out of the shower cubicle, the ring was bone-dry and once again quite comfortable on her finger.

The scene in the bedroom had affected everyone, and although they all tried to keep the birthday atmosphere going, they didn't quite succeed, so it was with some relief that Kate finally left to walk to her father's for lunch.

"Have a nice time!" called her mother. "And remember that you're going to that dance with Samantha and Clare tonight, so you'll need to be back by six."

"I know," replied Kate.

"Hope you get plenty of money!" Steve said with a laugh. Kate turned back to smile at him. *It's the least they can do, considering how little they have to see of her, the lucky swine!* she heard him add, yet his mouth was closed, and he was simply standing watching her go, his arm around her mother's waist.

The smile died on Kate's lips. This time she knew. There was no longer any point in trying to fool herself. She was hearing what people were thinking, and it had all started when she put on the ring. She was mortified to realize that Steve resented having her around the house so much and angry because it was her house after all. She'd lived there with her mum and dad right up till the divorce, and if anyone should feel resentful, it was her, not Steve, who'd not only moved in, but brought his daughters with him. Quickly, she ran through the gate and into the street.

All the way to her dad's house, Kate kept pulling hard at the ring, but it wouldn't move, and her finger was now red and sore. It was impossible to figure out how it had ever gone on that morning.

Lizzie was already waiting with the front door open when Kate got to the house. Jake and Ben were hanging onto their mother's skirt and stared at their big stepsister in their usual solemn way.

Lizzie smiled. "Happy birthday, Kate! Your father's just had to pop out for a moment. Have you gotten some nice presents?"

Kate nodded, disappointed that her dad wasn't there to kiss her and give her one of his warm, reassuring hugs, but she stretched out her hand and showed Lizzie the ring. "I got this," she said quietly, surprised to see that the ring looked quite loose and that her skin was no longer red around it.

Lizzie's eyes opened wide. "That's beautiful!" she exclaimed. As she bent down to pick up Jake, who'd started to whine, Kate heard her add, *God knows how they could afford that! Louise is always bleating that Brian doesn't pay enough child support for Kate, but that must have set them back a couple of hundred.*

Kate's lips tightened, and although she knew that she wasn't supposed to have heard, she couldn't help saying casually, "I saw it at an antique shop the other week, and it only cost twenty pounds."

"Really? That's amazing! It looks so real," said Lizzie's mouth, while Kate heard her add, *What a little liar she is. I suppose Louise told her to say that.*

Kate wanted to scream at Lizzie. She felt like telling her to stop saying one thing and thinking another because she could hear every thought that went through her head. Then she realized that it could be quite useful to be able to read people's thoughts. She'd always suspected that Lizzie didn't like her. Today she'd probably find out, and then she could confront her father with what she had learned. He was always saying that Lizzie liked her a lot, and he'd probably be shocked to find out that he was wrong.

At that moment his car pulled up, and he hurried toward her. "Happy sixteenth birthday, Kate! You're quite the young woman now. Don't you think she looks older, Lizzie?"

Lizzie laughed as they all went inside. "She got a beautiful ring from Louise and Steve," she said, her voice a little too bright. Kate showed the ring to her father. He leaned over her hand and examined it closely.

"That's quite a present! Make sure you don't lose it," he said slowly.

Kate felt like saying that she could hardly lose it when it wouldn't come off, and anyway she wasn't a careless person, but before she could utter a word, she was stunned to hear him thinking. *The next time Louise comes on the phone nagging for more money, I'll tell her to pawn the damn ring. What a stupid extravagance for a sixteenth birthday! No doubt Steve paid to show me up. Perhaps I should have gotten her more than thirty pounds from the bank just now. It's lucky the cash machine was working.*

There was real resentment in his thoughts, and Kate took a step away from her beloved father. Had he forgotten her birthday until this morning? Did he begrudge paying anything for her? And didn't any of them consider her feelings? She was beginning to think that she was nothing more than an expensive nuisance whom no one really wanted. Kate had never felt so alone.

At that moment Ben pushed himself forward and held out a card. "Happy birthday," he mumbled, while Jake hid behind him. Kate bit her lip to stop herself from crying, opened the card, and took out three ten-pound notes. She swallowed hard. "Thanks,

Dad. That's really generous. Thanks, Lizzie."

"We've got a tree house now—come and see," said Ben. Kate went willingly because she didn't think that she could look her father in the eye right at that moment. The tree house was a sturdy, well-crafted one set in the large oak at the bottom of the yard. "Only our friends are allowed in," said Jake.

"Am I your friend?" asked Kate and then wished the question unasked, but the two small boys nodded, and she heard one of them saying, *I love Katie.* She almost wept with relief and hugged them close, realizing gratefully that they were still too young to lie like the adults.

Lizzie had cooked Kate's favorite lunch: melon, followed by pork chops in cider and apples, with a sticky chocolate pudding to finish. Kate was now so terrified of what she might hear that she was afraid to make any kind of conversation, and if it hadn't been for the twins, it would have been a very silent meal.

*She gets more boring by the month*, she heard her father think as he lifted his glass of wine to toast her birthday. *I shall have to mention it to Louise. She doesn't seem to have any idea of how to chat or have fun.* He smiled at his daughter over the rim of his glass. "Happy birthday, sweet sixteen!"

Somehow Kate managed to smile back, but inside she was crying out with the pain of her father's betrayal. She'd always felt so secure in his love.

"Why don't you take Kate out for a walk this afternoon, Brian?" suggested Lizzie as she stacked the dishwasher. "The twins need a rest, and it would be nice for the pair of you to have some time alone together."

Kate watched her father carefully. His mouth smiled, but his eyes didn't as he nodded. "Sounds like a good idea. What about going along by the river? We could take the dog."

"Fine," agreed Kate apathetically, waiting for what was to come.

*At least the dog will enjoy itself,* she heard her father think as he took the leash off the peg in the hall. *The exercise will do Kate good too. She looks out of condition. I'll get Lizzie to tell her about that new aerobics class later.*

This was too much for Kate. "I'm not fat!" she shrieked, unable to bear it all any longer. "I'm perfectly fit. and I don't want to go for a walk with you ever again. I'm just sorry I cost you so much, but if I do badly on my exams, I'll leave school and get a job in a shop or something so that you can stop paying a penny, and then Jake and Ben can have another tree house or two with all the money you save."

Lizzie stood in the middle of the hall with her mouth open in amazement. "What on earth's going on?" she asked.

"I'm leaving!" shouted Kate. "I hate you, I hate him, and I loathe aerobics!"

"Aerobics?" asked a bewildered Lizzie. Her husband was too stunned by what his daughter had said to reply, but the loud slamming of the front door told him that Kate had really gone. He couldn't understand where all the anger had come from. Kate was normally so quiet. Nor could he figure out how she'd known anything about the aerobics, but assumed that Lizzie must have said something without him prompting her.

He sighed. Inside he felt rather guilty. Once he'd been close to his daughter, but now the twins took up most of his time and energy. They were a lively pair, full of chatter and much easier for a man to deal with than a withdrawn teenage girl.

"What happened?" demanded Lizzie more forcefully. "Did you say something unkind to her on her birthday?"

"No!" he replied testily. "I have no idea what got into her. It must be her age. All teenagers get moody. Anyway, she'll soon be back. She left her card and money behind."

Out in the street, Kate finally began to sob. Her tears just wouldn't stop, not even when people started to stare. She knew that she had to go somewhere, but she couldn't go home. She wouldn't give them the satisfaction of knowing that her visit to her dad had been less than perfect. Distraught, she decided to go to see Clare.

Luckily, Clare was in, doing her nails in her bedroom and listening to her favorite group on her CD player. "Hi! Happy birthday," she said casually and then looked at her friend more closely. "What's the matter? Didn't you get the ring?"

At that, Kate began to cry even more. The ring! She wished that she'd never set eyes on it. If only she could take it off, she'd throw it in the river and never ever want anything so badly again, but as she pulled on it, she felt the ring begin to tighten again, and her sobbing became hysterical.

Clare put her arms around Kate. "Hey, it can't be that bad. The ring looks great on you, and we're going out tonight. Is it your stepmother?"

"No, it's . . ." Kate couldn't go on. She couldn't begin to explain, because all at once she realized how stupid she'd sound. Clare would never believe that the ring enabled her to hear people's thoughts. Unless she showed her, thought Kate suddenly. If she got Clare to think of an object and then told her what it was, that would prove that she was telling the truth. "It's like this," she said between sobs. "I . . ."

*God, I hope she hurries up*, she suddenly heard Clare thinking. *Jeff's due here in half an hour, and she'll go crazy if she finds out that we're going out together, especially as she's hoping to go off with him at the dance tonight. How can I get rid of her?*

With a cry, Kate pulled herself free of Clare's embrace. "How could you?" she shouted.

Clare frowned. "How could I what?"

"Go out with Jeff. You are seeing him, aren't you?"

"Is that what this is about? No, I'm not. As though I'd do something like that behind your back! We're friends, aren't we? I know how much you like him, so why would I do something like that? Anyway, I'm going out with Mark at the moment."

Kate stared at her supposed friend. Clare's face shone with sincerity. She looked hurt and surprised, but not at all guilty, and the lies were flowing from her mouth so easily that Kate guessed that she must lie a lot. *Everyone lies*, she thought to herself. The man at the shop was right. She knew that now and knew too that she'd paid a high price for the ring, just as he'd said.

"Forget it!" Her voice was weary. "I'm going home now."

*Thank heaven for that!* thought Clare, while aloud she said, "Are you sure you'll be all right? I mean, you're welcome to stay for as long as you like."

"No, I've got to go."

"See you at the dance, then, around eight."

"I'm not coming," said Kate flatly. "I don't feel well."

"But it's your birthday," protested Clare, at the same time thinking, *Samantha will be relieved. Now we won't have to sit around keeping her company just because it's her birthday.*

"Would you tell Samantha for me? I hope she won't be too disappointed," said Kate, and she saw a faint flicker of disquiet in Clare's eyes.

"Of course; but she'll be really upset. It won't be the same without you."

"I know exactly how she'll feel," said Kate as she left Clare's room and trailed down the stairs.

When Kate got home, she told her mother that she thought that she had the flu coming on and went off to her bedroom. Louise took her daughter some hot lemon water and two aspirins and said what rotten luck it was on her birthday, but finally Kate was left alone, although not in peace. She'd had no peace since the ring went on her finger.

For hours she lay in her bed fiddling with it. It was no good. The ring wanted her as badly as she had once wanted it. Kate looked into a future where she would always know what people were really thinking. She knew that in the end it would drive her insane.

When Louise and Steve went to bed, Louise paid her daughter a final visit. "Daddy called earlier," she said, smoothing Kate's hair off her hot forehead. "He was very worried about you rushing off the way you did, but I explained about the flu, and he sent his love and said you must go by again as soon as you're better. Your money's still there."

"Right," mumbled Kate, keeping her eyes closed.

"You should have told him you felt sick," continued Louise. Kate didn't reply. Her mother's thoughts ran on. *How dare he criticize me because she's not very sociable? It doesn't come from my side of the family. His mother wouldn't step outside her own front door from one year's end to the other.*

*I hate them both,* thought Kate vehemently as her mother's thoughts continued. *Sometimes I wonder how I could have had such an uninteresting daughter. At her age I was always off having fun.*

"Good night," said Kate shortly.

"Good night, darling; I love you," said her mother gently.

It was an unbearable lie. Kate knew that she couldn't live like this any longer. No matter how difficult it proved to be, the ring had to go.

She waited until the house was silent and then crept down the stairs in the darkness and made her way through into the kitchen where all of the sharp cooking knives were kept. She'd get the ring off her finger if it was the last thing she did ...

It was her mother who found Kate lying dead and cold on the

kitchen floor the next morning. No one ever figured out what she was doing down in the kitchen in the middle of the night or how she came to sever the ring finger of her right hand almost in half with one of the kitchen knives, but in the end it was decided that it must have had something to do with her fever.

The actual cause of death was a combination of loss of blood and shock to the nervous system, and everyone was completely devastated. As an added mystery, no one was ever able to find the much-coveted birthday ring that had brought her—as her mother told everyone who'd listen—such happiness on her last day on Earth. They even tried to find a replacement to put in the coffin with her, but the jeweler's shop had closed down, and a large "Premises to Rent" sign was attached to the window.

On the very morning of Kate's funeral, as the stream of black cars followed the hearse to the crematorium, a young woman, Grace, wandered along the streets of a small town many hundreds of miles away, arm in arm with her new husband.

Grace knew how lucky she was. She'd married a handsome man who was rich and adored her. They stopped in front of a small, newly opened antique jeweler's shop, and Grace's eye was caught by a small gold ring with a beautiful ruby set in the middle, surrounded by tiny diamonds. It seemed to call out to her.

"Look, isn't that beautiful!" she said softly.

Her husband glanced down at her adoring face. He wasn't nearly as rich as Grace believed, but he had already insured his young wife for a great deal of money and was busy figuring out how to dispose of her without suspicion falling on himself.

"Would you like it, sweetheart?" he asked.

"Oh, yes! Yes, I would."

"Then let's go inside. If it fits, you can have it. I'd do anything to make you happy, Grace. You know that."

Grace glowed with pleasure, while her husband wondered how much the ring would cost and how soon he could put his plan into operation and collect the insurance money upon his wife's death.

They walked inside the shop. *Please let it fit*, thought Grace to herself.

A tall, dark man in his early 30s looked up and smiled at them. "How can I help you young people?" he asked gently.

# THE TROLL

### T. H. WHITE

"MY FATHER," SAID Mr. Marx, "used to say that an experience like the one I am about to relate was apt to shake one's interest in mundane matters. Naturally he did not expect to be believed, and he did not mind whether he was or not. He did not himself believe in the supernatural, but the thing happened, and he proposed to tell it as simply as possible. It was stupid of him to say that it shook his faith in mundane affairs, for it was just as mundane as anything else. Indeed, the really frightening part about it was the horribly tangible atmosphere in which it took place. None of the outlines wavered in the least. The creature would have been less remarkable if it had been less natural. It seemed to overcome the usual laws without being immune to them.

"My father was a keen fisherman and used to go to all sorts of places for his fish. On one occasion he made Abisko his Lapland base, a comfortable railroad hotel, one hundred and fifty miles within the Arctic Circle. He traveled the prodigious length of Sweden (I believe it is as far from the south of Sweden to the north as it is from the south of Sweden to the south of Italy) on the electric railroad and arrived tired out. He went to bed early, sleeping almost immediately, although it was bright daylight outside, as it is in those parts through the night at that time of the year. Not the least shaking part of his experience was that it should all have happened under the sun.

"He went to bed early, and slept, and dreamed. I may as well make it clear at once, as clear as the outlines of that creature in the northern sun, that his story did not turn out to be a dream in the last paragraph. The division between sleeping and waking was abrupt, although the feeling of both was the same. They were both in the same sphere of horrible absurdity, though in the former he was asleep and in the latter almost terribly awake. He tried to be asleep several times.

"My father always used to tell one of his dreams, because it somehow seemed of a piece with what was to follow. He believed that it was a consequence of the thing's presence in the next room. My father dreamed of blood.

"It was the vividness of the dreams that was impressive, their minute detail and horrible reality. The blood came through the keyhole of a locked door that communicated with the next room. I suppose the two rooms had originally been designed en suite. It ran down the door panel with a viscous ripple, like the artificial one created in the conduit of Trumpingdon Street. But it was heavy and smelled. The slow welling of it sopped the carpet and reached the bed. It was warm and sticky. My father woke up with the impression that it was all over his hands. He was rubbing his first two fingers together, trying to rid them of the greasy adhesion where the fingers joined.

"My father knew what he had to do. Let me make it clear that he was now perfectly wide awake, but he knew what he had to do. He got out of bed under this irresistible knowledge and looked through the keyhole into the next room.

"I suppose the best way to tell the story is simply to narrate it, without an effort to carry belief. The thing did not require belief. It was not a feeling of horror in one's bones, or a misty outline, or anything that needed to be given actuality by an act of faith. It was as solid as a wardrobe. You don't have to believe in wardrobes. They are there, with corners.

"What my father saw through the keyhole in the next room was a troll. It was eminently solid, around eight feet high, and dressed in brightly ornamented skins. It had a blue face, with yellow eyes, and on its head there was a woolly sort of nightcap with a red bobble on top. The features were Mongolian. Its body was long and sturdy, like the trunk of a tree. Its legs were short and thick, like the elephant's feet that used to be cut off for wastebaskets, and its arms were wasted: little rudimentary members like the forelegs of a kangaroo. Its head and neck were very thick and massive. On the whole, it looked like a grotesque doll.

"That was the horror of it. Imagine a perfectly normal golliwog (but without the association of a Christie minstrel) standing in the corner of a room, eight feet high. The creature was as ordinary as that, as tangible, as stuffed, and as ungainly at the joints: but it could move itself around.

"The troll was eating a lady. Poor girl, she was tightly clutched to its breast by those rudimentary arms, with her head on a level with its mouth. She was dressed in a nightdress that had crumpled up under her armpits so that she was a pitiful naked offering, like a classical picture of Andromeda. Mercifully, she appeared to have fainted.

"Just as my father applied his eye to the keyhole, the troll opened its mouth and bit off her head. Then, holding the neck between the bright blue lips, he sucked the bare meat dry. She shriveled, like a squeezed orange, and her heels kicked. The creature had a look of thoughtful ecstasy. When the girl seemed to have lost succulence as an orange, she was lifted up into the air. She vanished in two bites. The troll remained leaning against the wall, munching patiently and casting its eyes around with a vague benevolence. Then it leaned forward from the low hips, like a jackknife folding in half, and opened its mouth to lick the blood up from the carpet. The mouth was incandescent inside, like a gas fire, and the blood evaporated before its tongue, like dust before a vacuum cleaner. It straightened itself, the arms dangling before it in patient uselessness, and fixed its eyes upon the keyhole.

"My father crawled back to bed, like a hunted fox after fifteen miles. At first it was because he was afraid that the creature had seen him through the hole, but afterward it was because of his reason. A man can attribute many nighttime appearances to the imagination and can ultimately persuade himself that creatures of the dark did not exist. But this was an appearance in a sunlit room, with all of the solidity of a wardrobe and unfortunately almost none of its possibility. He spent the first ten minutes making sure that he was awake and the rest of the night trying to hope that he was asleep. It was either that, or else he was insane.

"It is not pleasant to doubt one's sanity. There are no satisfactory tests. One can pinch oneself to see if one is asleep, but there are no means of determining the other problem. He spent some time opening and closing his eyes, but the room seemed normal and remained unaltered. He also soused his head in a basin of cold water, without result. Then he lay on his back for hours, watching the mosquitoes on the ceiling.

"He was tired when he was called. A bright Scandinavian maid admitted the full sunlight for him and told him that it was a fine day. He spoke to her several times and watched her carefully, but she seemed to have no doubts about his behavior. Evidently, then, he was not badly insane; and by now he had been thinking about the matter for so many hours that it had begun to get obscure. The outlines were blurring again, and he determined that the whole thing must have been a dream or a temporary delusion, something temporary, anyway, and finished with so that there was no good in thinking about it any longer. He got up, dressed himself fairly cheerfully, and went down to breakfast.

"These hotels used to run extraordinarily well. There was a hostess always handy in a little office off the hall who was delighted to answer any questions, spoke every conceivable language, and generally made it her business to make the guests feel at home. The particular hostess at Abisko was a lovely creature into the bargain. My father used to speak to her a good deal. He had an idea that when you took a bath in Sweden, one of the maids was sent to wash you. As a matter of fact, this sometimes used to be the case, but it was always an old maid and highly trusted. You had to keep yourself underwater, and this was supposed to confer a cloak of invisibility. If you popped your knee out, she was shocked. My father had a dim sort of hope that the hostess would be sent to bathe him one day, and I daresay he would have shocked her a good deal. However, this is beside the point. As he passed through the hall, something prompted him to ask about the room next to his. Had anybody, he inquired, taken number twenty-three?

" 'But, yes,' said the lady manager with a bright smile, 'twenty-three is taken by a doctor professor from Uppsala and his wife—such a charming couple!'

"My father wondered what the charming couple had been doing while the troll was eating the lady in the nightdress. However, he decided to think no more about it. He pulled himself together and went in to breakfast. The professor was sitting in an opposite corner (the manageress had kindly pointed him out), looking mild and shortsighted, by himself. My father thought that he would go out for a long climb in the mountains, since exercise was evidently what his constitution needed.

"He had a lovely day. Lake Torne blazed a deep blue below him for all of its thirty miles, and the melting snow made a lacework of filigree around the tops of the surrounding mountain basin. He got away from the stunted birch trees, and the mossy bogs with the reindeer in them, and the mosquitoes, too. He forded something that might have been a temporary tributary of the Abiskojokk, having to take off his trousers to do so and tucking his shirt up around his neck. He wanted to shout, bracing himself against the glorious tug of the snow water, with his legs crossing each other involuntarily as they passed and the boulders turning under his feet. His body made a bow wave in the water, which climbed and feathered on his stomach, on the upstream side. When he was under the opposite bank, a stone turned in earnest, and he went in. He came up, shouting with laughter, and made out a loud remark that has since become a classic in my family. 'Thank God,' he said, 'that I rolled up my sleeves.' He wrung out everything as best he could, and dressed again in the wet clothes, and set off for the shoulder of Niakatjavelk. He was dry and warm again in half a mile. Less than a thousand feet took him over the snow line, and there, crawling on hands and knees, he came face-to-face with what seemed to be the summit of ambition. He met an ermine. They were both on all fours so that there was a sort of equality about the encounter, especially as the ermine was higher up than he was. They looked at each other for a fifth of a second without saying anything, and then the ermine vanished. He searched for it everywhere in vain, for the snow was only patchy. My father sat down on a dry rock to eat his well-soaked luncheon of chocolate and rye bread.

"Life is such unutterable hell, solely because it is sometimes beautiful. If we could only be miserable all the time, if there could be no such things as love or beauty or faith or hope, if I could be absolutely certain that my love would never be returned: how much more simple life would be. One could plod through the Siberian salt mines of existence without being bothered about happiness. Unfortunately, the happiness is there. There is always the chance (around eight hundred and fifty to one) that another heart will come to mine. I can't help hoping, and keeping faith, and loving beauty. Quite frequently I am not so miserable as it would be wise to be. And there, for my poor father sitting on his boulder above the snow, was stark happiness beating at the gates.

"The boulder on which he was sitting had probably never been sat upon before. It was one hundred and fifty miles within the Arctic Circle, on a mountain five thousand feet high, looking down on a blue lake. The lake was so long that he could have sworn that it sloped away at the ends, proving to the naked eye that the sweet earth was round. The railroad line and the half-dozen houses of Abisko were hidden in the trees. The sun was warm on the boulder, blue on the snow, and his body tingled smooth from the snow water. His mouth watered for the chocolate, just behind the tip of his tongue.

"And yet, when he had eaten the chocolate—perhaps it was heavy on his stomach—there was the memory of the troll. My father fell suddenly into a black mood and began to think about the supernatural. Lapland was beautiful in the summer, with the sun sweeping around the horizon day and night and the small tree leaves twinkling. It was not the sort of place for wicked things. But what about the winter? A picture of the Arctic night came before him, with the silence and the snow. Then the legendary wolves and bears snuffled at the far encampments, and the nameless winter spirits moved on their darkling courses. Lapland had always been associated with sorcery, even by Shakespeare. It was at the outskirts of the world that the Old Things accumulated, like driftwood around the edges of the sea. If one wanted to find a wise woman, one went to the rims of the Hebrides; on the coast of Brittany one sought the mass of St. Secaire. And what an outskirt Lapland was! It was an outskirt not only of Europe, but of civilization. It had no boundaries. The Lapps went with the reindeer, and where the reindeer were was Lapland. Curiously indefinite region, suitable to the indefinite things. The Lapps were not Christians. What a fund of power they must have had behind them to resist the march of mind. All through the missionary centuries they had held to something: something had stood behind them, a power against Christ. My father realized with a shock that he was living in the age of the reindeer, a period contiguous to the mammoth and the fossil.

"Well, this was not what he had come out to do. He dismissed the nightmares with an effort, got up from his boulder, and began the scramble back to his hotel. It was impossible that a professor from Abisko could become a troll.

"As my father was going in to dinner that evening, the manageress stopped him in the hall.

" 'We have had a day so sad,' she said. 'The poor Dr. Professor has disappeared his wife. She has been missing since last night.

The Dr. Professor is inconsolable.'

"My father then knew for certain that he had lost his reason.

"He went blindly to dinner, without making any answer, and began to eat a thick sour-cream soup that was taken cold with pepper and sugar. The professor was still sitting in his corner, a sandy-headed man with thick spectacles and a desolate expression. He was looking at my father, and my father, with the soup spoon halfway to his mouth, looked at him. You know that eye-to-eye recognition, when two people look deeply into each other's pupils and burrow to the soul? It usually comes before love. I mean the clear, deep, milk-eyed recognition expressed by the poet Donne. Their eye beams twisted and did thread their eyes upon a double string. My father recognized that the professor was a troll, and the professor recognized my father's recognition. Both of them knew that the professor had eaten his wife.

"My father put down his soup spoon, and the professor began to grow. The top of his head lifted and expanded, like a great loaf rising in an oven; his face turned red and purple and finally blue; the whole ungainly upper works began to sway and topple toward the ceiling. My father looked around him. The other diners were eating unconcernedly. Nobody else could see it, and he was definitely insane at last. When he looked at the troll again, the creature bowed. The enormous superstructure inclined itself toward him from the hips and grinned seductively.

"My father got up from his table experimentally and advanced toward the troll, arranging his feet on the carpet with excessive care. He did not find it easy to walk or to approach the monster, but it was a question of his reason. If he was insane, he was insane; and it was essential that he should come to grips with the thing in order to make certain.

"He stood before it like a small boy and held out his hand, saying, 'Good evening.'

" 'Ho! Ho!' said the troll. 'Little manikin. And what shall I have for my supper tonight?'

"Then it held out its wizened furry paw and took my father by the hand.

"My father went straight out of the dining room, walking on air. He found the manageress in the passage and held out his hand to her.

" 'I'm afraid I have burned my hand,' he said. 'Do you think you could tie it up?'

"The manageress said, 'But it is a very bad burn. There are blisters all over the back. Of course, I will bind it up at once.'

"He explained that he had burned it on one of the spirit lamps on the sideboard. He could scarcely conceal his delight. One cannot burn oneself by being insane.

" 'I saw you talking to the Dr. Professor,' said the manageress as she was putting on the bandage. 'He is a sympathetic gentleman, is he not?'

"The relief about his sanity soon gave place to other troubles. The troll had eaten its wife and given him a blister, but it had also made an unpleasant remark about its supper that evening. It proposed to eat my father. Now, very few people can have been in a position to decide what to do when a troll earmarks them for its next meal. To begin with, although it was a tangible troll in two ways, it had been invisible to the other diners. This put my father in a difficult position. He could not, for instance, ask for protection. He could scarcely go to the manageress and say, 'Professor Skål is an odd kind of werewolf, ate his wife last night, and proposes to eat me this evening.' He would have found himself in a loony bin at once. Besides, he was too proud to do this and still too confused. Whatever the proofs and blisters, he did not find it easy to believe in professors that turned into trolls. He had lived in the normal world all of his life, and, at his age, it was difficult to start learning afresh. It would have been quite easy for a baby, who was still coordinating the world, to cope with the troll situation; for my father, not. He kept trying to fit it in somewhere without disturbing the universe. He kept telling himself that it was nonsense: one did not get eaten by professors. It was like having a fever and telling oneself that it was all right, really, only a delirium, only something that would pass.

"There was that feeling on the one side, the desperate assertion of all of the truths that he had learned so far, the tussle to keep the world from drifting, the brave but intimidated refusal to give in or to make a fool of himself.

"On the other side, there was stark terror. However much one struggled to be merely deluded or hitched up momentarily in an odd pocket of space-time, there was panic. There was the urge to go away as quickly as possible, to flee the dreadful troll. Unfortunately, the last train had left Abisko, and there was nowhere else to go.

"My father was not able to distinguish these trends of thought. For him, they were at the time intricately muddled together. He was in a whirl. A proud man and an agnostic, he stuck to his muddled guns alone. He was terribly afraid of the troll, but he could not afford to admit its existence. All of his mental processes remained hung up while he talked on the terrace, in a state of suspended animation, with an American tourist who had come to Abisko to photograph the midnight sun.

"The American told my father that the Abisko railroad was the northernmost electric railroad in the world, that twelve trains passed through it every day traveling between Uppsala and Narvik, that the population of Abo was twelve thousand in eighteen sixty-two, and that Gustavus Adolphus ascended the throne of Sweden in sixteen eleven. He also gave some facts about Greta Garbo.

"My father told the American that a dead baby was required for the mass of St. Secaire, that an elemental was a kind of mouth in space that sucked at you and tried to gulp you down, that homeopathic magic was practiced by the aborigines of Australia, and that a Lapland woman was careful during her confinement to have no knots or loops about her person, lest these should make the delivery difficult.

"The American, who had been looking at my father in a strange way for some time, took offense at this and walked away so that there was nothing for it but to go to bed.

"My father walked upstairs on willpower alone. His faculties seemed to have shrunk and confused themselves. He had to help himself with the banister. He seemed to be navigating himself by wireless from the spot around a foot above his forehead. The issues that were involved had ceased to have any meaning, but he went on doggedly up the stairs, moved forward by pride and contrariety. It was physical fear that alienated him from his body, the same fear that he had felt as a boy, walking down long corridors to be beaten. He walked firmly up the stairs.

"Oddly enough, he went to sleep at once. He had climbed all day and been awake all night and suffered emotional extremes. Like a condemned man who was to be hanged in the morning, my father gave up the whole business and went to sleep.

"He was woken at midnight exactly. He heard the American on the terrace below his window, explaining excitedly that there had been a cloud on the last two nights at eleven fifty-eight, thus making it impossible to photograph the midnight sun. He heard the camera click.

"There seemed to be a sudden storm of hail and wind. It roared at his windowsill, and the window curtains lifted themselves taut, pointing horizontally into the room. The shriek and rattle of the tempest framed the window in a crescendo of growing sound, an increasing blizzard directed toward himself. A blue paw came over the sill.

"My father turned over and hid his head in the pillow. He could feel the domed head dawning at the window and the eyes fixing themselves upon the small of his back. He could feel the places physically, around four inches apart. They itched. Or else the rest of his body itched, except for those places. He could feel the creature growing into the room, glowing like ice, and giving off a storm. His mosquito curtains rose in its afflatus, uncovering him, leaving him defenseless. He was in such an ecstasy of terror that he almost enjoyed it. He was like a swimmer plunging for the first time into freezing water and unable to articulate. He was trying to yell, but all he could do was throw a series of hooting noises from his paralyzed lungs. He became a part of the blizzard. The bedclothes were gone. He felt the troll put out its hands.

"My father was an agnostic, but, like most idle men, he was not above having a bee in his bonnet. His favorite bee was the psychology of the Catholic church. He was ready to talk for hours about psychoanalysis and the confession. His greatest discovery had been the rosary.

"The rosary, my father used to say, was intended solely as a factual occupation that calmed the lower centers of the mind. The automatic telling of the beads liberated the higher centers to meditate upon the mysteries. They were a sedative, like knitting or counting sheep. There was no better cure for insomnia than a rosary. For several years he had given up deep breathing or regular counting. When he was sleepless, he lay on his back and told his beads, and there was a small rosary in the pocket of his pajama coat.

"The troll put out its hands to take him around the waist. He became completely paralyzed, as if he had been winded. The troll put its hand upon the beads.

"They met, the occult forces, in a clash above my father's heart. There was an explosion, he said, a quick creation of power. Positive and negative. A flash, a beam. Something like the splutter with which the antenna of a tram meets its overhead wires again when it is being changed around.

"The troll made a high squealing noise, like a crab being boiled, and began rapidly to dwindle in size. It dropped my father and turned around and ran wailing, as if it had been terribly burned, for the window. Its color waned as its size decreased. It was one of those air toys now that expire with a piercing whistle. It scrambled over the windowsill, scarcely larger than a little child and sagging visibly.

"My father leaped out of bed and followed it to the window. He saw it drop on the terrace like a toad, gather itself together, and stumble off, staggering and whistling like a bat, down the valley of the Abiskojokk.

"My father fainted.

"In the morning the manageress said, 'There has been such a terrible tragedy. The poor Dr. Professor was found this morning in the lake. The story about his wife had certainly unhinged his mind.'

"A subscription for a wreath was started by the American, to which my father subscribed five shillings; and the body was shipped off the next morning, on one of the twelve trains that travel between Uppsala and Narvik every day."

# Acknowledgments

The publisher would like to thank the copyright holders for permission to reproduce the following copyright material:

**Joan Aiken:** A. M. Heath & Co. Ltd. for "Something" from *A Fit of Shivers* by Joan Aiken (Victor Gollancz 1990), copyright © Joan Aiken Enterprises 1990. **Vivien Alcock:** John Johnson (author's agent) and Reed Consumer Books Ltd. for "A Change of Aunts" from *Ghostly Companions* by Vivien Alcock (Methuen Children's Books 1984), copyright © Vivien Alcock 1984. **Margaret Bingley:** Scholastic Publications Ltd. for "The Ring" by Margaret Bingley from *13 More Tales of Horror* (Scholastic Children's Books), copyright © Margaret Bingley 1994. **Philip K. Dick:** "Beyond Lies the Wub" by Philip K. Dick, copyright © Love Romances Publishing Company 1952, reprinted by permission of the author and the author's agent, Scovil Chichak Galen Literary Agency, Inc., New York. **Ellen Emerson White:** Writers House Inc. for "The Boy Next Door" by Ellen Emerson White from *13* (Scholastic Publications Ltd. 1991), copyright © Ellen Emerson White 1991. **Eleanor Farjeon:** David Higham Associates Ltd. for "Grendel the Monster" from *Mighty Men* (Basil Blackwell 1925), copyright © Eleanor Farjeon. **Nicholas Fisk:** Laura Cecil Literary Agency for "Teddies Rule, Okay?" from *Sweets from a Stranger* by Nicholas Fisk (Penguin Books Ltd. 1982), copyright © Nicholas Fisk 1982. **Leon Garfield:** Penguin Books Ltd. for "A Grave Misunderstanding" by Leon Garfield from *Guardian Angels*, edited by Stephanie Nettell (Viking Kestrel 1987), copyright © Leon Garfield 1987. **Terry Jones and Michael Palin:** The Gumby Corporation/Fegg Features Ltd. and Reed Consumer Books Ltd. for "The Famous Five Go Pillaging" from *Bert Feggs' Nasty Book for Boys and Girls* by Terry Jones and Michael Palin (Eyre Methuen Ltd. 1974), copyright © Terry Jones and Michael Palin 1974. **Stephen King:** Arthur B. Greene for "Here There Be Tygers" from *Skeleton Crew* by Stephen King (Futura Books 1985), reprinted with permission, copyright © Stephen King 1985. All rights reserved. **Jan Mark:** Murray Pollinger Literary Agency for "Nule" from *Nothing to Be Afraid of* by Jan Mark (Viking Kestrel 1980), copyright © Jan Mark 1980. **Guy de**